Richard Carpenter's

ROBIN OF SHERWOOD

THE RED LORD

by Paul Kane

Originally published in 2019 by
Chinbeard Books & Spiteful Puppet
in partnership with the
Richard Carpenter Estate
The edition published in 2021
www.spitefulpuppet.com

Layout & adaptation for this edition by
Andrews UK Limited
www.andrewsuk.com

CONTENTS

PROLOGUE

All was still in Sherwood.

Nothing was moving: there was no breeze in the trees; no animals in this part of the forest, or if there were they were remaining silent as well. Not even Robin Hood, standing and waiting, moved a muscle – in spite of the fact he'd hurried to this place. His breathing was slow, hardly noticeable at all; he'd long since learned how to control it, to move through the green like he wasn't even there, hardly making a sound. It was the only way to do what he did, to sneak up on the people that he robbed – giving the riches to those who really needed it. Or to evade capture, to stay alive.

Today he was doing neither. Today he'd answered the call, the same one he'd heard when he first came here. A voice he'd heard drawing him to Sherwood. To a spot not that far away, in fact, by the river. Where he'd been standing – hood up, concealing who he really was, an earl's son – and where he first saw a reflection of the person he'd eventually serve.

'I am Herne the Hunter,' a booming voice had told him then. A spirit, yet also a man, standing and staring at him from across the water. Not the same voice that had awakened him, and yet it was: 'Nothing's forgotten,' it had said. 'Nothing's ever forgotten.'

He'd been called to be Herne's son, a leaf on the wind. Called to do *His* bidding, to replace a legend, to save the followers of his predecessor. People he would grow to love himself, to call his friends. His family. As if in a trance, he'd strung the bow – giving it purpose, to prove himself. Then he'd rescued the others where they were being held captive in that hut in Wickham.

And then… then he had walked away from this life, something he still felt ashamed about if he was being honest with himself. He hadn't been strong enough to break the bonds of his upbringing, his duty, to leave his father and the castle. A mistake that had cost those followers – cost the people of this region – so dearly. A mistake he'd been trying to make up for ever since, to properly prove himself.

Which was why he always came immediately now when Herne summoned him. Not just because he was bound to this man, this spirit – his other father – but because he'd turned his back on his real birthright once, had sworn never to do so again.

And because usually it meant there was trouble.

Now, as he watched, Robin saw the familiar mist fill the clearing. It was why it was so quiet: here was a place of reverence, a bridge between his world and the one Herne occupied; the figure he'd first seen that day on the banks of the river merely a conduit between the two.

The mist was parting, revealing the shape of Herne; coming into focus and yet at the same time still dreamlike. The man he inhabited was like a giant once the spirit took hold, a mass of furs that seemed to flow into the ground itself. The stag's head he wore, complete with antlers, appeared to stretch into the branches of the trees, connected with Sherwood even more than Robin was: able to access the future as easily as he had just been recalling the past.

Robin's breathing hadn't simply slowed now, he was aware that he was holding that breath at the spectacle that always beguiled him. Still standing, still waiting for Herne to say something.

'My son,' came that same booming voice once more, filling his head and the clearing at the same time.

Robin nodded, finally letting out that breath and asking: 'Why have you sent for me?' His own voice, one that had given orders, that had led people into battle and persuaded yet others to alter their course, sounded weak by comparison.

There was a pause before Herne answered him this time, and Robin sensed a reluctance to impart whatever message he had for him. That could only mean something quite bad indeed.

'To deliver a warning,' stated the spirit. 'A time of darkness is upon us. A new enemy is about to make himself known. One who seeks to bring about eternal night, to spread terror throughout the land. One who seeks life never-ending.'

Robin frowned. 'Life never-ending? That's... that's not possible. Nobody lives forever.' Even as he said the words, he realised the irony of them. That Herne's son had 'come back from the dead' in another form – *his* form – that one day it might even happen again, perhaps long after he himself had passed and the Hooded Man was needed again. Yes, he was a very different Robin to the one that had gone before and yet the same. He also realised that he had heard…had *seen* stranger things during his time living in the forest.

More booming cut into his thoughts. 'He cannot be *allowed* to, or it will be the end of all things!'

Definitely bad. But it was about to get a lot worse.

'You must face him: one man of green against a man of red. Who is a *slave* to the red… Who is able to make puppets of men, leaving some of them damned beyond all hope.'

'I-I don't understand,' admitted Robin, letting his frustration show. Once again Herne was imparting something of great importance that might help with his task, but he always spoke in riddles – and very often the significance of what he'd said wouldn't become clear until afterwards.

'You will. But only after you have lost something you hold dear.'

Those words filled Robin with dread. 'Something I—'

'Remember!' Herne broke in. 'Only light can defeat the darkness, Robin. Only the light can save you… Save us all.'

It was something he'd heard before, that the powers of light and darkness were with him – held in balance, in check. It was knowledge, a responsibility that he was keenly aware of every single moment of the day. That it would only take something significant to tip the scales one way or the other. Something like this, actually.

But with the warning given, Herne was already withdrawing. Pulling back as if floating on the air, the mist covering his exit once more. Now Robin did move, rushing forwards, calling out: 'No, wait… Wait, tell me more!' It was already too late, however: Herne was gone and probably wouldn't be able to explain further even if he caught up with him. It was almost as if the details could only be fed to Robin in crumbs rather than the whole meal, the reason only becoming clearer as events played themselves out.

It left him with so many questions he couldn't answer: who was Herne talking about, the person who sought immortality? Who wanted to bring out permanent darkness? The red versus the green? Just *who* would he have to face?

But the warning had also left him with a fear that rocked the very core of him. At the notion he might have to lose something that meant a great deal to him before all this was over.

Something he might never get back.

That might never be replaced.

CHAPTER 1

Miles away, just outside Lincoln, out in the fields, it was the end of a very long working day.

The menfolk were returning home to their village after toiling away under the sun for hours and hours. Gathering the fruits of their labours not only to feed their fellow villagers, but to sell at the markets, to meet the demands of a greedy monarchy. It was well known that the war in Normandy was not progressing as King John might have liked, and the war cost money to fight, which meant, in turn, that the common people were taxed to the hilt. Sometimes they were left with nothing at all, as they had been last Winter when this particular community had almost starved.

Had it not been for Robin Hood and his band coming to their aid they might very well have done. The People's Champion, robbing from those who had more than they knew what to do with and distributing it amongst those who had nothing at all.

Jason, walking alongside a horse-drawn cart full of wheat, had often thought about a life like that himself. Maybe joining the outlaws if they'd have him, although he wasn't at all certain he was brave enough to count amongst their ranks.

Now his friend Thomas who he was travelling with, *he* was made of sterner stuff. A good head or more taller than Jason, the bearded man could carry twice as much and work three times harder without even pausing for water or rest. Thomas walked with his pitch-fork over his shoulder, whistling a tune; something that had stuck in his head from the last time they'd had a celebration.

It was around then Jason had last spoken of his desire to run off and fight with Hood's group – after a few too many ales probably – and Thomas had laughed, clapping him on the shoulder and calling him a dreamer. 'Why don't you just dream about Sal instead?' his friend had advised. 'Or, better yet, ask her to dance with you. She's been gazing over here all night!' And with that, Thomas had got up to dance with his betrothed, Mary, the flutes playing that tune he was still trying to whistle to this day.

Good advice, yet all Jason could think about was heading away from here for an honest to goodness adventure. But, as they were so fond of saying in these parts, you should be careful just what you wished for.

Because, as the sun dipped even lower that day and they were almost home – the women coming out of their huts to wave in greeting – Jason looked up and saw something on the hill that overshadowed their village. He squinted, then shielded his eyes with his hand. Framed against the red-orange of the sky, it was hard to make out exactly what it was: a dark shape that looked… that looked to have *wings*!

Jason elbowed Thomas, breaking into his whistling. 'Eh? What?' asked his friend.

He nodded towards the horizon, but when Thomas still didn't seem to understand Jason jabbed a finger in the direction of the ridge instead. 'Look!' he urged.

Thomas followed that finger, finally spotting the shadow there which was getting bigger by the second. His brow furrowed, obviously just as puzzled by the shape, and he transferred his pitch-fork from one shoulder to the other.

'What *is* that?' said Jason, more to himself than anyone.

Thomas was scratching his head with the hand he'd just freed up. 'I… I confess I'm not rightly sure.' He was squinting as well now, trying to get a better look at the thing. 'Some sort of bird?' Thomas offered with shrug.

'A *giant* bird?' Jason replied, because that was what it looked like, flapping those wings as if it was about to take off. But no, the more they both stared, the more they realised it couldn't be a bird – not unless that huge bird knew how to ride a horse.

'It's a man,' stated Thomas. 'See, that's his cape flapping behind him.'

They could hear the hooves now of the steed he was on, like thunder in the distance. If they thought the man was big, then the beast he was riding was even bigger – it had to be to accommodate his bulk. It might have been a trick of the light, but both appeared to be the same colour as that boiling crimson sky, as if they had ridden directly out of it. Or perhaps they had flown, thought Jason, to land on that hill – though it might have been more appropriate if they'd tunnelled up from below, out of Hell itself.

As massive as they were, they were getting larger all the time, descending that slope, giving the impression of swooping once more. Then all of a sudden an object was held out to one side, long and pointed. Something the rider was gripping firmly as he drew closer and closer still.

Jason swallowed dryly when he recognised what it was. 'An' he has his sword drawn!' Managing to tear his eyes away from the scene, he gripped Thomas just as firmly by the arm. 'Warn the others. He means to attack!'

But there was no time. The horse and its mount had covered the remaining distance in no time at all, ploughing into a group of men off to their right. It knocked them over, this way and that, like a ball being rolled at some skittles in a child's game.

It didn't end there, though: Jason gazed in horror as a man called Enoch, still on his feet, felt the bite of that steel the man was swinging. The blade tore right through the poor unfortunate, cleaving him in two with a spray of dark redness. The rider seemed to be trying to steer into that jet before it abated, bathing in it almost as one might do to cool down on a hot summer's day when a shower finally rained down. Here it was raining onto his winged helmet, splattering the flesh of his chin – the only part of his face exposed, apart from the slits across the eyes.

The rest of the figure wore armour as well, Jason couldn't help noticing. It shone in what was left of the light, which glinted off those smooth surfaces like an insect's shell. He couldn't tell now whether it was because of the blood, or it had always been scarlet, but it was definitely red in colour. A red... knight? Cape still flowing out from behind him, his horse also sporting a dark red caparison which covered it.

When the man finally dismounted, Jason got a sense of just how enormous he was. A giant! Much bigger even than Thomas, he looked several times stronger as well. That wasn't stopping his friend from rushing to help their fellow villagers, pitch-fork now in both hands and raised like a weapon.

'Thomas! Wait!' Jason shouted after him, but the bearded fellow was taking no notice; definitely the braver of the two of them. And that bravery was about to put him in terrible danger.

Thomas swung his makeshift weapon and the knight simply held up his forearm, letting it crash against it, the wood splintering in every direction. Growling, Thomas raised his fists, but the knight just cocked his head, fixing his opponent with a stare that stopped him in his tracks. At first it looked like Thomas was resisting, but then the knight grabbed him by the neck, almost lifting him and bringing their faces closer together: that incredible vision appearing to bore into his friend.

Thomas screamed suddenly, all of his courage forsaking him in that moment. When the knight pulled back again, dropping him, Thomas' whole body went slack as if all the life had fled from it. Had he broken the man's neck? There was another cry from behind and Jason turned to see Mary watching from the settlement, yelling for someone to help Thomas. Her love was beyond help, however, falling to his knees before keeling over sideways.

'*Run!*' someone else shouted off to the side of Jason. 'Run, before he—' The man's words were cut off along with his head, which went flying into the distance.

Jason was suddenly aware of the horse that had been pulling the cart, rising up on its back legs and neighing in fear at the giant's approach. It tried to get away, dragging the cart off with it, but only succeeded in pitching the whole thing sideways which pulled the horse to the ground as well, legs kicking out like an upturned spider. Wheat was spilling everywhere, but that was the least of their concerns at the moment. You couldn't eat or sell that if you were dead.

All around him was chaos. Men running back and forth in a panic, some trying to get away then stopping and gaping at the knight when he turned his sight upon them. He ran some through, others he left to stand, mesmerised, and still more he would grab by the neck, snapping sideways before flinging the body away like a doll, accompanied by deep-seated laughter. It was hard to work out just what the purpose of all this was – if there even *was* a purpose.

And then, finally, it was Jason's turn. The helmeted figure spotted him and fixed him with a gaze that turned all of his limbs to lead. He couldn't move at all, but at the same time found he didn't really want to.

'Come,' said a voice – the knight's voice, a Lord no less... His Lord. But he was speaking without even moving his mouth, the words echoing inside Jason's head. 'Join me. You want adventures? I promise they await if you come with me.'

It was like he was in a dream... A dreamer, that's what Thomas – poor lifeless Thomas – had called him. No, this was more like a nightmare. More like—

But Thomas was getting up now, rising. Regardless of the state he'd been in, his friend was coming on the adventure as well.

'Join me!' said the voice once more, persistent, unwavering, and Jason nodded emphatically this time. How could he possibly resist? Those eyes, that voice. The promise. 'Good, good. You belong to me now.'

Jason and Thomas were walking again, in the opposite direction to the village. Past bodies that were never going to rise again, like the decapitated man. Following the call, joining their Lord who was mounting up again and sheathing his mighty sword.

In his dreamlike state, he was aware of more screams from behind them, one of them Mary's, who couldn't understand what was happening: was Thomas alive, was he dead... or somewhere in-between? How could she possibly understand?

Not like Jason, for he understood it all now his new master had explained it to him. He hadn't needed words in the end, it had all just become so clear. He knew what he had to do and where he had to go.

Wherever his Lord and master was going.

***

Sal was pulling Mary back, though she herself wanted to follow more than anything in this world.

Mary wanted to follow Thomas, and she Jason. But Sal recognised how dangerous that would be. The corpses scattered out there on what had become a battlefield told her that if nothing else. No, not battlefield. It had been a slaughter, pure and simple.

Their men, the men of the village, killed. All except the handful that were leaving with the person who had done this. Who'd flown down that hill and done his worst with that sword of his, with those eyes.

'Thomas!' Mary was shouting. '*Thomas!*' She tried to break free from Sal, but her friend held on to her tightly. They'd lost so much already today. Mary turned to her, wide-eyed – confusion in those eyes. And terror. 'Thomas, James, Gregory... Your Jason. Where are they all going, Sal? What's the matter with them?'

She shook her head, as much because Jason wasn't hers – not yet. Not like Thomas was betrothed to Mary, but she'd like him to be. 'I don't know,' she said honestly. 'I don't know.'

Mary began to cry then, collapsing into Sal's arms, sobs wracking her body. 'Why?' she kept asking, over and over. 'Why?'

As Sal watched the handful of figures vanish over the hill, striding after the rider on horseback, she could only shake her head again and wonder.

Wonder where they were all going, what would happen to them when they got there.

And what would happen next.

CHAPTER 2

Nottingham Castle.

It had sat, immovable, since William the Conqueror first laid the foundations and over time it had become one of the most important geographical sites in England. Near to the River Trent and on the central road to the North it was perfectly positioned and heavily fortified, something that hadn't seemed to stop Robin Hood and his band getting inside on several occasions. Using their cunning and guile during one such recent incident, they'd even made off with 60,000 marks in taxes that the King was due to personally collect. It was one of the reasons the guard had been doubled of late, why there were two men rather than one at the gate standing and watching the approach of the riders on horseback in the far distance.

The sky was growing darker, in spite of the fact it was only the middle of the day, and Henry – one of the guards on duty there – commented that it looked like a storm was due. That was all they needed, standing outside; they'd get drenched. It would also account for the reason the riders, a handful of them, were speeding up.

But to Cedric, the other guard standing on the opposite side of the entrance, it didn't look like they were trying to beat that storm at all. More that they were bringing it with them, the blackness rising at their backs.

Then suddenly they'd arrived at the castle itself and the sky was darker than ever. Like a shroud had been pulled over the top of them all, over the building and the walls surrounding it, but there was still no sign of the rain. Cedric counted them, though he'd never been very good at counting, and settled for there being about a dozen. All wearing polished black armour the likes of which he'd never seen before, which made them look for all the world like giant beetles.

Only the man at the front wore something different. His armour was red... dark red in colour, his helmet sporting strange wings on either side. The cloak he had on flowed down and over the horse he was riding, feeding into the maroon covering the animal. Though he looked for it, Cedric could see no markings, nothing to give away the allegiance of these soldiers. For that's what they certainly were, he could tell not only by what they wore but the way they carried themselves even when mounted. Bolt upright, alert. They'd drawn up sharply at the gates, as if waiting to be admitted without question. But the guards had their orders and the Sheriff would have their guts for garters if they disobeyed.

'W-Who goes there?' Henry called up to the men, one hand on his pike, the other on the hilt of his sword. He couldn't prevent the hitch in his voice, however, which betrayed his nerves. When no answer was forthcoming, Henry grabbed the pike with both hands and waved it in the general direction of the newcomers. 'I asked you a question. Identify yourselves!'

The man in red, the largest of them all and most solidly built, looked not at Henry but Cedric and when those eyes locked on to him, it felt like they were penetrating his very soul, as if there was nothing he could hide from the fellow. Not even the fact he himself had been pilfering from the castle kitchens. Still a thief, as he had been when he'd been conscribed; not much separating him from Hood's men apart from ambition.

At that precise moment, Cedric could think of no good reason why these men *shouldn't* pass through into the castle grounds. Indeed, he felt so strongly about it, that he turned and made to start opening the gates.

'Cedric?' asked a bewildered Henry. 'Cedric, whatever are you doing?'

It felt very much like a stupid question to Cedric: what did it *look* like he was doing? Opening the gate up so these noblemen could enter and go about their business. But Henry was intent on stopping that from happening, stepping towards Cedric in fact – forcing him to shove Henry backwards. It looked like he was going to try again, but then froze on the spot. He too had now caught the giant man's gaze and was simply standing there as if he'd forgotten what he was about to do next.

Not that it mattered, because the gate was open now and the riders were urging their horses to move forwards, to follow their leader. All Henry could do was watch as they went by, as Cedric nodded to each one in turn, welcoming them to Nottingham Castle.

***

7

'You stupid woman, look what you've done!'

Sir Guy of Gisburne had leapt up from the bench as soon as he felt the wetness on his tunic. The serving wench had spilled the wine she was pouring into his goblet, the clumsy imbecile, and were it not for his lightning fast reflexes the accident would have been much worse. As it was, most of the claret had ended up either on the table in front of him or on his clothes.

He ignored the fact that it was getting so much darker in the castle's great hall – not that it was ever really light inside that large, stone room – the fact that this servant was probably having difficulty seeing what she was doing and the fact that she had clearly been shaking even before he began shouting at her. The servants here were all trained to be afraid of their masters as soon as they began to toil for them. There was no excuse for such an outrage!

'I should have you flogged!' barked Gisburne, which was something he always enjoyed doing to the hired help anyway. The woman looked like she was about to burst into tears, but was biting them back, knowing she would only make things worse for herself. Gisburne couldn't help smirking. He'd see those tears, before he was finished with her… *If* he was able to see anything at all that was! 'And *why* is it so dark in here all of a sudden?' he bellowed, head snapping from side to side, taking in more members of staff that were present. 'Light more candles immediately! Did you not hear me, I said light more—'

A noise interrupted his rantings, the loud creaking of heavy wood and metal ahead of him. There were two ways into the great hall at the far end: a small archway on the left with a flight of steps; and a set of high double doors directly in front. And it was the latter that were opening now, both sides flung back to reveal a number of armoured men standing in the entranceway. No-one had announced them, they weren't expecting visitors, so the only conclusion Gisburne could draw was that they were intruders at the castle. Soldiers who had fought their way inside and were intent on causing trouble.

'What's the meaning of this?' he demanded. 'Who are you people? How did you get in here?'

There was no reply. He asked again, but still none of the men spoke. Gisburne was used to being ignored by those of a higher rank than him, but if there was one thing he simply wouldn't tolerate it was a snub from complete and utter strangers who didn't even know him.

The servant girl forgotten about, he set off to cover the ground between him and the trespassers. As he ran, he drew his sword, clutching it with both hands. Not one of the armoured men moved an inch; it was like they barely considered him a threat – and that just made him even angrier.

'Gisburne! Gisburne!' The call came from behind him, a voice he recognised at once. A voice he himself had been trained to obey, if he knew what was good for him. 'Put that thing away before you do yourself a mischief!'

He halted, drawing up short before he could reach the men. And it was only now – in the light the candles there were throwing back – that he took in the strangeness of their armour. Black and shiny, except for the huge man at the front whose winged helmet was almost brushing the uppermost point of the archway. His armour was red, a very dark shade of red.

He stared at them for what seemed like forever, only wrenching his head back to address the person who'd called him off when said person coughed. The small man who must have entered from the back of the room while Gisburne was readying to attack. He stood on the plinth where his 'throne' was, dressed in the finest dark green cloth trimmed with gold – illuminated by the extra candles that were now hurriedly being lit in the hall. His jet-black hair was receding – even more so at the moment due to the problems he'd been facing – but the colour matched that of the hair under his nose. In the past he'd favoured a beard, but he'd had that cut back into a moustache which he liked to stroke when he was deep in thought… usually plotting something. His eyes were bulging with excitement, and that told Gisburne the man had probably been plotting again. Perhaps these men might be part of that very plot.

'My lord…?' he queried.

'They're *here* because I sent for them,' Robert de Rainault, the Lord High Sheriff of Nottingham, informed his aide. 'That is, I sent for *him*.'

The Sheriff pointed a gloved finger at the giant in red. The largest of the group, who was stepping forward as he was being addressed, nodding to the left and right for his men to remain where they were. Only one came close to being as tall as him, but even then it was no contest.

The giant strode past Gisburne without even giving him a glance.

'Indeed, I thought there *was* only you,' the Sheriff said, once the man was closer, having negotiated his way along the makeshift aisle the tables on either side of the hall created.

'There was,' a powerful, rumbling voice answered, which suited the figure down to the ground. This was all he would disclose by way of an explanation and the Sheriff's right eye half-closed, as it was wont to do when he was annoyed. It soon opened again when the man facing him removed his helmet, revealing hair that was even darker than the Sheriff's, but much longer and tied back in a ponytail. His skin was ashen, verging on white, as if he hadn't been outside in a very long time. Or just hadn't taken off his helmet.

'But... but who *is* he?' Gisburne couldn't keep the exasperation from his voice as he trotted up to join them, putting his sword away at the same time.

'A warrior from the east. Someone who might actually rid me of that infernal Robin Hood and his outlaws once and for all!' The Sheriff's fists were opening and closing at the very mention of his dreaded enemies, who'd slipped through their fingers more times than they cared to admit... though somehow it always ended up being Gisburne's fault. People who had obviously made the Sheriff so desperate he was once again bringing in outside help, just as he'd done before, only to watch those plans fail as well. It was thinking about this that jogged Gisburne's memory, however. That caused him to piece it all together and work things out, even before the Sheriff's next few words. 'Allow me to introduce you. This,' the small man continued eventually, 'is Lord Dragos. More commonly known as—'

'Dragos the Red,' Gisburne finished for him, which would ordinarily have warranted a harsh word or two for interrupting. This time the Sheriff merely raised an eyebrow. 'Also called The Red Lord,' Gisburne added, though the large man's lip curled at the use of that particular name.

'So, you've heard of him then?' replied the Sheriff, taking his seat on the golden chair behind him. When he leaned back, the round section at the top made it look like he had a halo – though Gisburne couldn't imagine anyone less saintly if he tried.

'I have,' he answered, skirting around the side of the larger man. How could it have been anyone else? he asked himself. It was obvious now that he thought about it. 'A fighter with a ferocious reputation. A once noble lord who ruled his Kingdom through fear and strength in numbers, but lost it all and had to resort to becoming a mercenary in order to survive.'

Dragos grimaced and rounded on Gisburne, looming over him. This time he backed up a little; a reflex action, Gisburne told himself afterwards, and nothing more. He wasn't afraid of this... this brute. Not really.

'Lord Dragos, please accept my sincere apologies,' said the Sheriff, leaning forwards. 'Gisburne doesn't mean any harm by his words. He can't help being an incompetent buffoon! But I assure you, he's really not worth the effort.'

The bigger man relented, nodding his acceptance. Gisburne let out the breath he hadn't realised he'd been holding. A buffoon, was he? Incompetent? He wasn't the one who'd turned to a madman such as this, with his reputation. If the Sheriff was even aware of those rumours that was, those legends about this monster? Wouldn't be the first time, of course, that he'd allied himself with those who were known to dabble with the forces of darkness. Why, the very first time he and the Sheriff had encountered Hood – the one from

Loxley – and his band, they'd thrown their lot in with a man people said was a sorcerer: the late Baron de Belleme, involved in all kinds of black magic. Gisburne had been present when the Sheriff had made a deal with that fellow, had seen the distaste de Rainault's brother Abbot Hugo had displayed at the very thought of it all. He absently wondered now what that holy man might make of this. Would he consider the risk acceptable to get rid of the thorn in their side at long last?

'My lord, I—' Gisburne began, an attempt to try and counsel the Sheriff.

'Oh, do be quiet, will you!' was the reply he got back, so he thought the better of it. He'd only be inviting more insults. 'Now,' the Sheriff continued, 'let us turn our attention to business. Are you quite sure you can help me with my little... problem?'

'I can,' Dragos assured him. 'For a price.'

The Sheriff hesitated briefly then. It was always the same when the subject of parting with money cropped up, but in the end he said, 'Naturally... naturally. Everything has its price, Lord Dragos. You do this for me and you will be handsomely rewarded.'

A grunt, followed by another nod. 'Then it is settled,' Dragos told him. 'The wolfshead and his wolves will bow to me... or they will die!'

Gisburne folded his arms: he'd heard such promises before. Only this time... Maybe, just maybe... What worried him however were the Sheriff's own words, rolling round and round in his head now: Everything has its price.

Everything has its price.

CHAPTER 3

It was night-time in the forest.

Robin was gazing into the fire they'd used to roast their evening meal. Or more accurately that Tuck had used to roast it, the smell of the meat still lingering. Sometimes the ex-Friar complained about being the one who did all the cooking, but everyone knew deep down he really enjoyed it. Food was one of the most important things in the world to Tuck, the great love of his life after God and religion. Indeed, apparently he'd spent most of his time at Thornton Abbey when he was training to be a monk in the warming house or the kitchens.

'My,' said Little John not far away, laying on his side with his head propped up on his hand, 'that was a nice bit a venison. A meal fit for a king, in fact!'

'Well, one certainly provided the ingredients,' replied Will Scarlet with a chuckle, sitting upright with his elbows resting on his knees, picking bits of food out of his teeth with a fingernail.

'Aye,' John replied with a laugh. 'Washed down with some ale, you can't beat it. And compliments to the cook, of course!'

Tuck smiled at this, chest puffed out with a swell of pride. 'You're very welcome,' he told them with a smile.

Much, the lad Robin had watched turn into a man before his very eyes – had practically been one when he first met him – was smacking his lips. 'Is… is there any more?' he asked.

'Any more, he says!' Scarlet laughed again, shaking his head. 'Wanting seconds… or is it thirds? You're beginning to sound like 'im.' Removing the finger from his mouth, he prodded it in Tuck's direction.

Tuck frowned at this remark, then shrugged, conceding the point. 'Was rather nice, if I say so myself. Though on this occasion, I'm absolutely stuffed.' He patted his round belly to demonstrate. 'I'm not sure I'll ever eat another thing.'

'Now *that* I would like to see!' When Scarlet guffawed this time, the others joined in. The famous outlaws gathered together and living in Sherwood, fighting the good fight. To give hope to the common people, oppressed by the likes of the Sheriff. To stand up for them when no-one else would.

He'd done that, Robin reminded himself. He'd brought them back together again, after he'd come to his senses and returned to Herne. They'd been scattered, were disillusioned after the death of their former leader. How much easier it would have been if he'd just stayed behind after freeing them, after firing that flaming arrow into the water. Nevertheless, he'd gone to them and had to prove his worth to each in turn. With Tuck, a battle of wills – finding him in Sherwood and convincing him to take them to John and Much in Hathersage. Those two had been living simple lives as shepherds and he'd needed to goad Little John into fighting him with the quarterstaff; the first step along the way of gaining his trust.

From there, he'd tracked down Scarlet – who'd been spending his days getting drunk in his brother's ale house. Robin had to prove himself that time with his fists, a brawl through the streets that had only ended when the Watch had been summoned. Scarlet had said back then and many times since, if he hadn't been the worse for alcohol he would have beaten Robin, but neither of them had ever been in a hurry to test that with a rematch.

All people he held dear. Was it one of them he was destined to lose?

And then there was Marion, always Marion. Robin's eyes flicked over to her now, laughing with the rest of the band. Eyes sparkling, hair the colour of those flames he'd been staring into. So beautiful... He'd fallen in love with Marion the first time he'd clapped eyes on her. Had known she was the love of *his* life when they'd danced at a feast his father, the Earl of Huntingdon, had prepared. She'd been there with her own father, and Robin... Robert back then... had warned Marion about the designs that Welsh monster Owen of Clun had on her – then soon realised she could take care of herself. That only made her all the more attractive in his eyes.

It seemed so long ago and at the same time like it had happened yesterday. He'd proved himself to them all, gone on to continue earning their respect. He remembered the first time one of them had called him 'Robin' – Little John it had been. And the first time one of the people had, blessing him because the man in question had been about to have his hand cut off. Then there was the sword he'd inherited, Albion: one of the powerful swords of Wayland. He'd resisted taking it at first because he hadn't felt himself worthy of the weapon, but it had chosen *him*. Shown Robin was its master by not slaying him. He wondered absently if it was Albion he was going to lose.

Robin recalled Marion asking at the start of all this whether he thought they'd accept him as their leader. His reply had been: 'Would you?' As a leader and… perhaps more? It hadn't been long before she'd returned to the forest to be with her friends, and he'd gotten his answer to the first part as she'd fought alongside him time after time. But the more time they'd spent together, the closer they'd become as well. He felt the love there, every time she held his hand, or the first time they'd shared a kiss in the back of that hay-cart escaping from King John's clutches. He'd admitted that he'd been jealous when he saw her in the royal bedchambers, and that's when it had happened: their kiss. The most magical moment of his entire life…

And not that long ago, the joyous time they'd spent with the Sheriff's young nephew Martin in the forest, after getting him away from Adam Bell. They'd played games with him; she'd taught Martin how to shoot a bow and arrow. They'd had fun – and that had made him wonder about a life with Marion. Perhaps a family, beyond the one they already had in Sherwood… (If that was at all possible for people like them, and he wasn't destined to become like Bell himself.)

Yet still she held back. He knew the memory of his predecessor lingered, haunted her. Made her wary. He'd never wanted to take *his* place, he couldn't, because he was his own man – yet Robin couldn't help how he felt. As much as she was frightened of losing him, of history repeating itself, maybe she was the one Herne had been—

'What do you think, Robin?' Her voice now, so sweet and gentle. Asking him a question, and he realised he hadn't really been listening to anything in the camp for some time.

'Hmm?' he replied.

There was concern etched on that beautiful, freckled face of hers now as she repeated what they'd been talking about, how they should probably all cut down a bit on their portions of food. John had once said that he'd never eaten as well since he became an outlaw and was now joking they'd have trouble scrambling up trees or running away from trouble soon if they weren't careful. 'Oh… oh yes, probably.'

'Not him,' said Tuck, nodding at Robin's plate. 'He's barely eaten anything tonight.'

'What is it, Robin?' Marion asked him outright now. 'What's the matter?'

'You've not been yourself since you came back from seeing Herne,' said Much.

'Why won't you tell us what 'e said?' Scarlet shook his head. 'I dunno. What's the big secret?'

'There's no secret, Will,' Robin maintained. Yet how could he tell them he was about to lose something, some*one* he loved? Or perhaps whatever was going to happen would break them up, maybe it was that he was destined to lose? The closeness, the togetherness of this? Scarlet was shaking his head again, flapping a hand to say it didn't matter; as if to suggest he was always keeping things from them. Perhaps *not* telling them would be how he lost their trust anyway? 'No secret. Not really... It's just—'

He was interrupted by a noise, a rustling of tree branches and foliage. Everyone sprang to their feet, in spite of the food they'd been eating. Scarlet had said to Robin when they first met that they weren't sharp anymore as a team, but they were sharp enough now – out of shape or not – as swords were drawn and arrows primed.

They relaxed almost as one, though, when they saw it was the missing member of their band. Nasir, the Saracen – or to give him his full title, Nasir Malik Kamal Inal Ibrahin Shams ad Duala Watthab ibn Mahmud – clothed in black and dark brown, crossed swords at his back and throwing daggers on his shoulders. It had been a stroke of luck that Robin had encountered him the first time, a coincidence... except nothing ever happened by accident, he'd soon learned. In Clun's fighting pit, he'd proved himself to this fellow with his skills as a swordsman – taught to him by the guards at Huntingdon, just like the quarterstaff. And, same as the rest, Nasir now followed Robin without question.

He'd been on lookout tonight and his face was sterner than usual. 'What is it, Nas?' asked Little John.

A man of few words, the Saracen replied in his usual clipped way: 'Men. On horseback.'

Then he beckoned for them all to follow *him*.

***

Nasir had been right. As he motioned for them to crouch down and said, 'There!' they saw for themselves several riders moving slowly along the dirt track that ran through the very heart of Sherwood.

Robin had lost count of the number of rich travellers they'd robbed on this stretch, leaping out from the bushes or jumping down from the beeches and the oaks that flanked it. The amount had tailed off in the months since the Hooded Man had returned to Sherwood, but even when people did frequent this place they did so in the daytime. Nobody, absolutely *nobody* came here at night.

Yet here these people were. Several of them, wearing armour the colour of Nasir's clothes – darker even. And a much larger figure at the front, bigger and wider than the rest: he was head to toe in red, which could be seen clearly in spite of the dimness.

One man of green against a man of red, thought Robin.

'Soldiers? In Sherwood? At night?' Turning to the rest of them, Scarlet couldn't hide the surprise on his face. 'Are they mad?'

'They're either very brave,' said John, 'or very, very foolish.'

'Maybe they thought it would be safer?' Marion offered.

'Well, they were wrong.' Scarlet was starting to rise.

'Wait!' Robin told him, grabbing his arm.

'*Wait?* Wait for what?' demanded Scarlet.

But Robin didn't have an answer for him. Not until he saw their leader climb down from his steed, heard that voice ring out: 'I know you're out there!' When the man spoke it was with authority, and even though he wore a helmet it felt like he was looking through the darkness right at the group. 'Robin Hood! Surrender now and spare yourself the pain of defeat!'

'Spare ourselves... Someone's a bit big for his boots,' said Tuck.

'Bit big for *everything*,' Scarlet observed. 'Look at the size of 'im!'

You must face him...

Robin screwed up his courage. He hoped it wouldn't come to that. '*You're* the ones in our territory and surrounded! We have our arrows trained on you.' He nodded and Marion let one fly, which embedded itself in a trunk not far from the man in red.

'Impressive,' came the reply, which seemed to be aimed solely at the shooter. 'But the darkness is my territory! And are you *quite* sure about who is surrounded?'

There was a rustling nearby, and this time it wasn't Nasir.

'Robin!' shouted Much. 'Look!'

'His men are everywhere!' Scarlet said through gritted teeth. 'All around us!'

'It's a trap!' Little John swung his staff at the nearest approaching foe, who toppled sideways but soon righted himself again.

Then the forest erupted around them, at least twice as many men again as there were down on the path suddenly attacked from the other three sides: left, right and behind, those black knights were everywhere! There was the clang of metal on metal, as Robin countered the swing of a sword, shrugging it off, before meeting another.

'Look out!' cried Tuck, and Scarlet ducked to avoid a swipe from another blade. Nodding his thanks to the holy man, he rose and batted away the sword. Nasir had his swords crossed to block an incoming blow from above, kicking the soldier back once he'd trapped the sword with his own.

'There, Marion.' Little John pointed. 'Shoot!'

She pivoted and let off two arrows in quick succession. They found their marks, hitting one soldier in the leg, another in the arm; both in the tiny gaps between the armour. It would have stopped most fighters in their tracks, but these opponents didn't even seem to notice.

Much swung his slingshot around his head and let fly with a stone. It struck its target, but simply bounced off the armour – so he got down low and rolled, taking the man's legs out from under him and causing him to roll down the hill to the path below. The figure just got up again, readying himself to return.

''Ere, have some of that!' shouted Scarlet, jabbing at one of the soldiers and finding a soft-spot himself between the armour. The blade went in a good few inches, but nothing happened. Confused, Scarlet yanked it back out and tried again. Still there was no response.

Nasir was having the same difficulty. He'd slashed one of the soldiers across an exposed bit of his flank, had thrown a dagger at another and watched as it hit home – but neither slowed down his opponents.

'It's... It's like they can't even feel it!' cried out John, catching one in the stomach to double him over, then crashing his quarterstaff down on the back of his neck.

Scarlet exchanged glances with him. 'What's... what's goin' on?'

Robin slashed at the fighter he was tackling, again with no reaction.

One who is able to make puppets of men... He heard Herne's voice as if he was speaking to him right here and right now. Then he looked down and saw the giant standing by his horse and watching this battle, directing his troops. 'He's... They're all under his control!' he exclaimed. Then he knew what he had to do. 'The leader. I have to face him!'

'*No!*' shouted Marion, firing off a couple of more arrows. Again, they hit their marks – in the gaps between metal – but didn't fell the soldiers.

'It's suicide,' Tuck agreed, barging into one of the soldiers and sending the man flying.

'I have to try,' Robin said, then was sliding down towards the path. He skidded the last bit, tumbled and found himself on the ground not far away from the leader. From that angle, looking up, the man appeared bigger than ever! Robin scrambled to his feet, Albion at the ready.

The giant nodded, then pulled out his own sword. That too was larger than Robin's weapon, with what looked like a spiked hilt. 'So, you are the one they call Robin i' the Hood.'

'A-And you are?' He tried to hide it, but Robin was terrified. How was he supposed to fight this… this mountain of a man? He was taller even than Little John! It was David and Goliath all over again. *But remember what happened to Goliath*, Robin said to himself. Perhaps he should have borrowed Much's sling?

'Me? I am your doom. I am your end,' spat the man in red. 'I am your death.' With the last few words said, he swung his sword.

Robin gripped Albion with both hands, held it up to block the attack – and was almost knocked off his feet again. He felt the vibrations run all the way up his arms and into his shoulders, which sent everything numb for a few moments. Somehow, Robin managed to push the sword, and the man wielding it, back. But almost immediately, his enemy swung again. This time Robin pitched sideways to avoid the blade. He felt the air part, heard the swish of the blade which would have sliced him in two.

Once, twice, three times more, Robin met the blows with Albion. 'You're getting tired, little man!' The giant swung again, and again. There was no opening for Robin to retaliate.

He ducked and rolled now, as his opponent's sword struck the ground only a whisper away. But Robin couldn't avoid the kick that sent him over and over. Now he was on his back, and the giant in red was standing over him, raising his sword. He'd been right all along: this was his end, his death.

He closed his eyes, knowing what would happen next. That he was about to lose something dear to him… his very life!

Only the next thing he heard was the familiar sound of arrows flying. Robin snapped open his eyes, saw projectile after projectile strike the giant – causing him to shield himself with one arm, to pull back from the killing blow. Marion! Marion had saved him!

Stones followed next, then a dagger, then blows from swords and a quarterstaff.

His friends had joined him, leaving the other soldiers behind – and were distracting the giant. Suddenly Robin was being helped up to his feet; Scarlet and Nasir on either side of him, dragging him away to the other side of the path. 'The river,' Little John – off to his left – was saying. 'We need to make for the river!'

They were all running, but Much had stumbled on the road. Tuck turned, saw what had happened. 'Oh no…' The miller's son had basically taken Robin's place on the floor, and was a sitting duck for the giant's blade. Much looked more petrified than even he'd felt: eyes wide and staring up at the man in red.

Robin shrugged off his companions and rushed back. He reached out for Much, grabbing him by the wrist and pulling him out of harm's way – then did what the others had done for him, getting the lad to his feet.

'You came back for me,' said Much.

'Of course!' Robin told him. He wasn't losing anything… *anybody*, today. Glancing back, he saw that the rest of the black knights on the incline – plus those on the path – were massing. The giant was climbing back onto his horse, preparing to give chase. 'Now let's go!'

Much and Robin raced through the undergrowth, trying to catch up with the rest, all the time aware that they were being followed. Being hunted.

By the time they reached the river, the others had almost made it across. Robin urged Much on ahead, then sheathed Albion and waded into the water himself, only turning when he was over halfway – looking back to see where the giant and his men had got to.

They were at the water's edge, the horses rearing up and refusing to cross. The giant too was gesturing for them all to hold back, regarding the river with a sneer. Was it Robin's imagination, or did he seem scared to cross?

Then the giant looked up and found Robin again. 'Until we meet again, Hooded Man!' he shouted. And suddenly he was turning his horse around, the rest of his men – on foot and horseback – doing the same.

Robin watched them depart, before swimming the rest of the distance to the other shore. 'Come on, come on!' Scarlet was saying to him, having already helped Much out of the river. Robin clasped his hand, welcoming the help once more.

'Where are they going?' asked Tuck, puzzled.

'Is that it then?' This was John. 'They're just leaving? Is it over?'

Robin shook his head; he doubted very much that any of this was over, especially after what the giant had said by way of a farewell. But they were all safe for now, he hadn't lost any—

'Wait,' said Robin, spinning, desperately looking around him at them all. 'Where's Marion?' He'd thought he saw her running, but in the confusion and darkness had lost sight of her. Had one of the giant's men grabbed her?

There was someone behind him, a hand on his shoulder. 'I'm right here, Robin. I'm fine.'

Robin turned, couldn't help the smile that broke on his face. And couldn't help opening his arms to hug her, to hold her tightly to him. After a moment or two, however, she pulled free, her eyes brushing the forest floor.

'Who *were* they?' asked Scarlet. 'That's what I want to know?'

'Who was *he*?' added John, referring to the leader.

All Robin could do was shake his head again, recalling those other words the man had said to him.

'I am your doom. I am your end… I am your death.'

And he had a horrible feeling that it wouldn't be long before they found out.

CHAPTER 4

Who was he? Who was he *really*?

He'd often thought about this, particularly in his time moving from place to place – the length of the journeys encouraging contemplation. Not that he was in a rush as such, he would have all the time in the world soon. Had lived for so long already.

Once he'd been the ruler of a kingdom, a lord, with a castle and armies at his beck and call. Even before, he'd had power. It had been because he wanted to hold on to that power that he'd made the bargain, and because he'd been promised much more power besides. His enemies had been growing in number and he had to do something to stamp on them before he was overthrown.

And so, the pact. The deal with the forces of darkness that had filled him with black magic; that had given him his strength, his longevity, his… abilities. Once he had opened himself up to the possibilities, he'd found himself drawn – directed – to a forest similar to the one the Hooded Man called his home. A dark place the locals called haunted, filled with spirits. There – in the very centre of the place – he had encountered something he couldn't describe. A force: evil in its purest form. He had been so, so frightened when it came to finally going through with his end of the agreement. But by that time it was way too late to do anything about it. Even if he had run, a pitiful attempt to hang on to his old life, his 'innocence', it would have caught up with him and taken him anyway. As it was, he was too scared to even move when it filled him up.

When it awoke something inside him.

It was the last time he could recall ever experiencing fear. As the blackness took him, moulded him. Gave him knowledge most men could only dream of.

It let him go eventually and he stumbled from the forest, emerging and squinting at the sun above. Somehow he knew it would not kill him, but nevertheless it weakened him, that light; the opposite of the dark. He was far stronger in the shadows, which was why the forces he had conspired with aided him in this respect, clouding over the sky wherever he went. One day, if he – and they – had their way, that darkness would be permanent and he would be forever. It was something they were working towards even today.

With each step he took back towards his castle, he felt more and more powerful. He was able to stand up straighter, and as tall, as well-muscled as he'd been before, he was even more so after his encounter with the evil. A gargantuan, a colossus. Able to influence people with a stare – ensuring his reign – and destroying others' minds completely, tearing their very souls apart. He built an army, in addition to his personal guard who would die for him unconditionally and were filled only with his will and black magic. But even without them, he was strong enough to lay waste to his enemies, growing to enjoy the slaughter at close quarters. The bloodshed. And for a time all was well, but he was unaware of a conspiracy amongst his own people. That holy men were being consulted and their actions would ultimately lead to his downfall, to his personal guard being obliterated (put out of their misery, they'd called it) and those he'd merely influenced coming to their senses. That not only would it eventually end in him being driven out of his own kingdom, but measures would be put in place so that he might never return again.

He'd wandered then, exiled and aimless: the lust for power and bloodlust still alive in him; killing as a way of life, essentially. As a way of taking out his frustrations on mankind – something he no longer felt a great connection to – and as a way of getting some kind of revenge. It had also proved quite lucrative, hired by those who had need of his talents: a mercenary employed by Kings and Lords with problems like those he had faced himself. He'd fought wars that were nothing to do with him, deposed other leaders and changed the landscape of entire nations. If King Richard, or his brother John after him, had asked then he could probably have settled their troubles overseas within weeks, if not days… For a price, of course.

The fact was, his lifestyle wasn't cheap. Hedonistic in the extreme, he still enjoyed the finer things in life and they cost money, especially if they weren't strictly legal. It was why, when the Sheriff made it known that he wished to open a dialogue, the call had been answered… and answered in person. He'd known what it was pertaining to, naturally. Stories about the Sheriff of Nottingham and his arch enemy Robin Hood had spread not just throughout England, but across oceans as well. It was only a matter of time before he was

approached. Before the Sheriff's desperation brought the man to his door...
or vice versa.

On his way there, he thought it would be a good idea to at least start to build
his numbers. But he'd enjoyed the attack on that village more than he thought
he would. Favouring some, purging them of their essence – the strongest
amongst them...physically at any rate – and adding them to the ranks of his
new personal guard, who would later be clothed in black armour he'd bought
with what was left of his monies. Beguiling others, acolytes who would serve
as cannon-fodder where necessary in his larger army. The rest he'd simply
enjoyed butchering, the screams of their kinfolk back at the settlement like
music to his ears.

It was actually on his way to Nottingham Castle, and his encounter with
the Sheriff himself – not to mention his halfwit lackey, who he'd almost killed
just for being so insolent – that he'd struck upon the notion. That perhaps
he might be able to make a new home for himself here, somewhere he could
take over and rule. Somewhere to build a new kingdom for himself. He hadn't
needed to 'persuade' the Sheriff to part with an initial sum to initiate this
plan; the man had practically been begging him to deal with his problem.

As he'd assumed: Hood and his band of outlaws who, it had to be said,
hadn't been as easy to annihilate as he'd thought. Their reputations were
warranted, he had to admit. The way they'd fought against his 'chosen' had
been admirable, the courage Hood himself had shown commendable. Had
it not been for the river they'd crossed, cutting them off, the job would have
been finished that night. As it was, and as he had explained to the Sheriff
in his report, he had given them pause for thought. Left them not knowing
where or when he would strike again, simply that they would. And he had left
them with a little surprise...

'I didn't ask you to *unnerve* them, I want them all dead!' the Sheriff had
told him, that right eye of his turning into a slit.

'In time,' he'd explained. 'All in good time.' Then he'd gone on to explain
his plan to dismantle Hood's support mechanisms, namely striking at the
heart of those villages who gave him aid – who, in return, Hood aided. It was
a sound plan, but one which at the same time would swell his own ranks. He
looked back now, over his shoulder as he rode, to see exactly how much they
had grown since he'd been here. How the numbers had increased, spreading
like a plague: his chosen ones, and the beguiled.

All his playthings.

All heading now to a new location, a base from which they could mount
yet more attacks. As it had been with the dark forest, something had drawn

him – or even directed him – to this place. A feeling, a calling he couldn't explain even if he'd tried. Travelling east again, but to the coast this time.

And there it was, an abandoned castle – a fortress – that had once been the seat of a very different kind of power. Evil had dwelt here once a long time ago and been snuffed out, but he could still feel its energy. A perfect place for his own kingdom to thrive. He'd purchased the lands with the money the Sheriff had given him already, though more had been promised.

As they entered through the dilapidated gates which would be the first thing that needed fixing – shoring up the defences something of a priority – he already felt like he was home. That this place would *become* his true home after so many years of being a nomad.

There was just one thing missing now, but again – he reminded himself – that would also come in time. He would make sure of that, and events were already in motion that would give him what he desired.

So, he asked himself again: who was he? The Sheriff's fool had called him 'The Red Lord', a name he had always despised, in spite of the fact he had courted it with the colour of his armour. Some called him 'The Dragon', again because of his name and because of his cloak, the winged helmet – mythical creatures that spat fire and had scales. He'd been called worse than either of these: much, much worse.

Who was he? He was blood royalty, he was a prince, a king. He was Dragos, and the whole of this isle would tremble soon at the very mention of that name.

He was Lord Dragos, soon lord of all he surveyed, master of men.

And there was no force in Heaven nor Hell who would be able to stop him this time.

CHAPTER 5

'He's gettin' worse, I'm tellin' you!'

Robin hated to admit it, but Scarlet was right. Notorious for overreacting to anything such as this – like the time he'd thought he might have leprosy and they'd all had to make the pilgrimage to Croxden Abbey, where the fabled healing cross of St Ciricus was housed – Robin had to concede that this time the spiky-haired man leaning against a tree at their new temporary camp had a good point.

Much had been with Scarlet that day as well, when they'd both eaten food they later thought might belong to lepers – only for them all to discover it was Gisburne and his men in disguise; some kind of scheme to steal the cross for whatever vile reason. The former miller's son had dealt with all that much more calmly than Scarlet, in fact the latter had ended up being held hostage by Sir Guy because he went after him in that same hot-headed way which always got him into trouble.

Sadly, Much wasn't even awake at present to deal with whatever this was. He'd fallen ill not long after their encounter with what they were calling the 'Red Giant', which could hardly have been a coincidence. They'd regrouped, hiding out at the Major Oak till morning came, not that the morning, nor any of them since, had brought much by way of sunlight… The skies today remained, as they had done back then, overcast, as if they were living under constant threat of a storm that never appeared. None of them had ever experienced weather like it, not even John when he'd been looking after those sheep in Hathersage. 'Unnatural!' was what he called it and Robin had to agree. Something else they had to thank the Red Giant for, the first stages of what Herne had been warning about: the unending darkness.

Discussing what had happened, post-battle, they'd come to the conclusion that the men they'd fought – those black knights – had been far from natural as well.

'I mean, I know they had armour on and everythin', but I cut them… I ran one of 'em through!' That had been Scarlet as well. 'Nas did some damage too, I saw 'im. Didn't you, Nas?'

The Saracen had nodded. 'Al-ghul,' stated the man then.

'What does that mean?' asked John.

'Not living,' Nasir clarified, then shook his head to try and put it better. 'Living, but not *alive*.'

'You mean like those things we fought near Crom Cruac?' chipped in Tuck. Robin's mind flashed back to that encounter, where he'd tackled figures in black robes brandishing scythes; like the village itself, which had originally burnt to the ground a century before, it had all been tied in with the sorcerer Gulnar's spells. Thankfully, that villain was gone now… though not a day had gone by since that incident that Robin hadn't wondered if he was gone for good. And what might happen if he returned. But that was for the future, they had more immediate problems to deal with.

'I don't think they were the same, these men were more… solid,' stated Robin. 'The others vanished when you wounded or… or killed them, if that's the right word. But Herne did say something about the damned. That the man of red could make puppets of people.'

Scarlet had held up his hands. 'Oh, now 'e tells us! You let us sit there munching on that venison when Herne had been warning you about damned men who might attack!'

'He didn't say they *were* going to attack, Will. Or when.', Robin sighed. 'You know how this works, how open to interpretation it all is.'

'Open to interpretation? Open to interpretation! How much more interpreting do you need than what just 'appened?'

It was always the way with Scarlet, who loved nothing more than a good argument or to complain about something, who sometimes forgot who the real leader was. John put a hand on Scarlet's shoulder to calm him. 'Easy lad, it's not Robin's fault, all this.' Scarlet sucked in a huge breath, then let it out again slowly and nodded, visibly relaxing.

But maybe it had been his fault, though, thought Robin. Maybe Scarlet *was* right and he should have said more about it, instead of keeping things from the group, keeping them in the dark. And by the time he was ready to share, the giant and his men were already in the forest. If he hadn't been thinking about what he would have to face, what he might lose… He still hadn't said anything about that to his companions. Wouldn't telling them something like that only worry them? Affect how they fought?

'They seemed to shy away from my cross,' Tuck said, to fill the silence that had descended, and referring to the emblem of his faith he wore around his neck. 'As if they were scared of it. Nothing on the side of good would be frightened of that!'

'Well, we *know* they're not on the side of good, Tuck,' Scarlet piped up again, directing his annoyance at that man now. 'You could tell by the way they were tryin' to kill us!'

'Did you see their eyes?' This was a lighter voice, a woman's – and they all turned to look in Marion's direction.

'What's that?' asked John.

'They were blank, like they were empty inside – not really people at all. Like there was nothing inside them but… but whatever that giant had put in there.'

Tuck frowned, as if piecing things together. 'There are tales, just stories really. Rumours from other countries, from foreign parts.'

'That accent of 'is was definitely not local,' Scarlet observed.

Tuck ventured on in spite of the interruption. 'Rumours about men who have been taken over, who have no souls anymore, no minds of their own. Vessels really for something else, controlled by the blackest of magics… Some say they can't even *be* killed.' Robin bristled when he heard that, Tuck echoing Nasir but also Herne's words about immortality. 'Cursed, damned… Whatever you want to call it.'

'Never mind about all that, how do we fight 'em?' Scarlet wanted to know.

Tuck shrugged. 'They're just stories, like I said. But in those, fire sometimes works. Silver perhaps?' He held up his cross again.

Scarlet threw up his hands again in despair. 'Sometimes works…? Per'aps?'

It was getting them nowhere, the discussion going round in circles – and they were all very tired. Even before the fight, they'd been tired, readying to bed down for the night. So, once the area had been checked, and taking turns to keep watch, they tried to get some sleep.

It was easier said than done, however. Robin was restless, kept closing and then opening his eyes, replaying the earlier events in his head. Much muttering in his sleep hadn't helped either. He'd never had any trouble drifting off, that lad – and talking to himself wasn't that unusual an occurrence. Even a raised voice once or twice, which had caused the whole camp to wake, they'd put down to what had happened with those men in the forest. Much probably wasn't the only one to have nightmares that night.

Except, when they woke the next morning, he looked worse than some of the group who'd hardly slept a wink. He had dark bags under his eyes and was complaining that he didn't feel right.

'Probably all that venison last night,' John had joked, ruffling his hair.

They hadn't thought anything of it, really. Not even as they came up with a plan to find out what was happening – Tuck volunteering to go out there, visit Nottingham maybe, speak to people out in the villages. As well as being the cook, he very often also stood in for their scout; folk opened up more to a holy man, was what he always said: 'Probably the overwhelming urge to confess.'

'I dunno,' John had said. 'Could be dangerous.'

'I'll blend in, same as always,' Tuck promised him. 'It'll be fine.'

'I don't mean the Sheriff's men…'

'Well, our new "friends" could be anywhere. They could come back here at any time,' Tuck pointed out, which did little to boost their spirits. 'And we need to know more about them. I'll return before too long.'

Robin himself was reluctant to let him go, especially given what Herne had said, but he recognised the wisdom of gathering information. And as he'd said, it might be safer out there than in the forest at the moment. So the ex-Friar set off, walking with his staff through the green until he disappeared.

Thinking about what Tuck had said, they decided to move around themselves, never staying in one place for more than a few hours and keeping vigilant all the time in case of another attack.

'They didn't exactly sneak up on us, though, did they?' Scarlet had said. 'Didn't seem to care whether we saw 'em or not. Coming down that path, large as life.'

'Would you care,' was John's reply, 'if you couldn't feel pain? If you were that hard to kill?'

'The ones that surrounded us did a pretty good job of sneaking about. None of us saw a thing,' Robin reminded them both, then glanced over at Much. 'Still not feeling so good?'

Much had a pained expression on his face, and shook his head. He'd been unusually quiet as well, for him. When Robin asked him to describe it, Much just said again that he didn't feel right.

'Perhaps a chill from the river?' suggested Marion. 'Do you ache at all, Much?'

He shook his head again, but then almost stumbled as they made their way to the next fresh camp. Nasir caught him before he toppled headfirst to the ground. 'He is sick,' said the Saracen in his usual gruff tones, telling them what they already knew.

Marion suggested that they make camp before long, just so Much could rest, and he fell asleep again practically as soon as he lay down in the grass. This time there was screaming rather than just muttering and a raised voice. He was sweating as well, but when Marion felt his brow she said he didn't feel hot at all. 'There's no fever,' she told them from her crouched position beside him, a puzzled expression on her face.

'Check 'im,' Scarlet told her, which drew another frown from her. 'Check 'im for y'know, signs that he's damned.'

'Like what?' asked John.

Scarlet shrugged. 'I… Marks or somethin', signs that they could 'ave passed somethin' on?' They'd all heard what Tuck had said about a curse, what Robin had told them about Herne's warning. None of the others had been affected, but it was definitely better to be safe than sorry. Anything could have happened in the confusion of that skirmish, the ensuing fight above the pathway.

There were no visible marks anywhere, on the parts of Much that were exposed like the arms or chest. At one point he woke up and grabbed Marion's wrist as she was pulling up a sleeve. His eyes were wide, and he demanded to know what she was doing.

'We need to work out why you're feeling ill,' Robin explained to him, and he seemed to calm down at that point, letting her get on with the examination. In the end she looked back over her shoulder and shook her head. There was nothing. 'I'll mix up some herbs to soothe him,' she said, rising. Marion was the closest thing they had to a healer; she'd even managed to cure Robin that one time when he'd been hit by a poisoned crossbow bolt.

It wasn't long after Much had consumed this – Marion getting him to chew on a concoction of her devising, which did seem to help it had to be said – that there were rumblings about moving again. 'We've been 'ere too long,' Scarlet said, eyes darting left and right. 'We should keep goin'.'

He wasn't wrong, of course, it was just that Marion was concerned about Much's condition. 'I don't think we should move him.'

'Well, we can't leave 'im 'ere!' argued Scarlet.

'I'll help him,' said John, placing an arm under his shoulder, practically lifting him off the ground as they went.

They did this for some time, moving around so that the enemy couldn't find them if they came back – but leaving signs for Tuck to follow if he did. With each day that passed, however, they began to wonder if he ever would and at the same time Much's mystery malady was growing worse.

'I'll bet you anything this is down to that… that thing in the red armour,' John said after easing Much down this final time. He hadn't really woken up since Marion had looked him over, not for any length of time at any rate. Scarlet had suggested that perhaps she'd given him too many of those herbs, which had earned him a stern sideways look. But Robin was inclined to agree with Little John; this was definitely the Red Giant's work somehow. If nothing else, it had divided the group – kept them occupied and unable to even think about striking back at Red and his men.

It was as they were pondering what to do next that they heard yet more rustling in the undergrowth. Seconds later, Tuck came crashing through gasping for breath. 'Water, water...' he managed. 'I'm fair parched.' They might not have seen the sun for some time, but all of them agreed it was getting warmer in the forest – and Tuck had just made a long journey, longer even than they realised, as it turned out.

'We were beginning to worry.' Robin gave him water from one of their skin-pouches, enough for him to tell them where he'd been and what he'd discovered. Not just Nottingham, but a tour of various villages in the area.

'And what I learned was it's down to the Sheriff, all this,' he puffed and spluttered.

'Of *course* it is!' said Scarlet, turning away and rubbing the bottom of his chin. 'It's always 'im!'

'Not always,' John replied, then thought about it. 'But very often, aye.'

'Let him speak,' Robin said, holding up his hand to quieten them.

'Anyway, he's brought in outside help... because of us. Seems he's more anxious than ever to get rid of Robin Hood and his outlaws.'

'He just might succeed an' all,' Scarlet couldn't help adding, before Robin shushed him.

'A warrior. A warlord from the east. Dragos his name is, Lord Dragos. Some call him Dragos the Red, or just the Red Lord.'

The Red Lord, thought Robin. Not as descriptive as Red Giant, but somehow suited the man perfectly. The way he carried himself spoke of nobility, which was something that had also been said of himself.

'Yes, but what's he doing *here*?' John queried.

'I'm getting to it, I'm getting to it,' Tuck snapped. 'The Red Lord lost everything apparently, was driven out of his kingdom. His homeland. He's hired muscle now.'

'A mercenary?' said Scarlet.

'He's more than that,' Robin promised. 'Much more.'

Tuck nodded. 'That's how the Sheriff heard about him, anyhow. His reputation precedes him.'

'*I've* never 'eard of 'im,' Scarlet insisted.

'This is deadly serious, Will,' said Tuck.

'You think I don't know that?' He pointed back to the forest, not necessarily in the right direction but to illustrate his next few words. 'We were lucky to get out of there alive! And look at Much...'

Tuck was silent for a moment or two; since he'd returned he hadn't really taken the sight of the young man in: still out cold on the floor, but restless, thrashing around. 'They say he has certain powers,' said the holy man then.

'Who says?' asked John.

'The people at the villages I called at. That's what I've been trying to tell you, if you'll let me.' Tuck exhaled loudly, then drew in another deep breath. 'We're not the only ones he's been menacing. He's been busy, has our Red Lord. Newark, Retford... villages all over. And where he's visited, he's devastated them. Men have just gone off and joined him, maybe because they're scared or because of something else... Some have been killed and some who appeared to be dead have just got up again and joined him.'

'The black knights,' said Robin under his breath.

'He'll have many more besides since we encountered him. And he shows no signs of stopping, either.'

Robin banged his fist against his leg. 'We should have been there, we might have been able to prevent this. Those people needed us and we failed them.'

'We didn't know,' Tuck said to him. 'And we can't be everywhere at once.'

'He's building an army,' said John. 'But... but that can't just be to get us, surely?'

'People have come after us with more,' Marion observed. 'And we've got the better of them.'

'What's he up to?' Little John mused, stroking his thick beard.

'What's it matter? We 'ave to stop him before this all gets out of 'and.'

Robin rounded on Scarlet. 'And how do you propose we do that, Will?'

He opened and closed his mouth a couple of times, thought about it, then said: 'Well, I dunno, do I!'

'That's what I thought.'

Scarlet clicked his fingers. 'Herne! Go back and see what 'e has to say about it.'

Robin knew what Herne would say, the same as last time. That he should face him, his opposite number – and was he starting to see parallels here between them, former titled men who'd lost everything? No, Robin had gained so much more than he'd lost. He'd *gained* everything when he came here. Robin wasn't prepared to lose it, either.

Before he could reply to Scarlet, there was more movement in the foliage. This time they all grabbed their weapons, ready in case it was the Red Lord and his men rampaging through Sherwood looking for them. Instead, it was Nasir – just like it had been the first time. But he wasn't alone.

With him was a young boy, no more than about ten. They all recognised him instantly as young Matthew, Edward and Alison's son. It explained why Nasir hadn't alerted them ahead of Tuck appearing, he'd been busy trying to calm Matthew down, bringing him to them.

'Matthew,' said Robin, 'what is it?'

Tears were streaming down his face as he attempted to explain what was wrong, but struggled to get it out. Luckily Nasir stepped in and put it simply: 'Men. At Wickham.'

'The Red Lord's men?' asked Robin, then realised Nasir hadn't been there when Tuck had told them his title. 'The Red Giant?'

A curt nod was all he needed. Wickham had been good to them in the past, in fact some might say of all the villages they helped it had become their favourite – that they knew the people there better than anywhere. That had its drawbacks, of course, one of which was it made the place a target for those who wanted to hurt them, wanted to draw Robin and his band out. Nevertheless, they had to answer the call.

'We might not be able to be everywhere,' he said, looking at Tuck as he said it, 'but we can be in Wickham right now. We can prevent them from doing to that place what they've done to all those others.' Robin sheathed Albion and grabbed his bow.

'We can stop this from getting any worse,' he stated finally, with an emphatic nod.

CHAPTER 6

Edward stood waiting outside his hut, arm around his wife Alison.

She was shaking, and he was doing his best to assure her that everything would be all right. But how many times in the past had he done exactly that, only for things to go spectacularly wrong, largely because of their association with Robin Hood? The last time had seen some of their number rounded up, Alison included, and thrown in the dungeons at Nottingham Castle when Philip Mark – the 'Butcher of Lincolnshire' – took over briefly as Sheriff and threatened to kill them if Robin and his people weren't delivered. The plan had almost succeeded as well.

Then there was the time the whole village was occupied by the Sheriff and his soldiers, when they'd hunted down and captured all the outlaws except Much and Marion… and Robin, of course. The *first* Robin. The man those same soldiers had killed in cold blood, made such a mess of him he was unrecognisable. A hooded man they'd thought had returned from the grave when he rescued them, tied up with a guard on watch in a hut only a stone's throw away from where Edward was right now.

But that hooded man had been Robert of Huntingdon, an Earl's son… He'd come to Edward as well, a year after those events, claiming that he was also Herne's son. That he was here to do the spirit's bidding. Here to make a difference once more. And he hadn't let them down: they were all still here in spite of the hardships they'd endured, and a lot of that was down to Robert… Robin. Definitely Robin.

It was who they turned to first in situations such as these. Why Edward had sent his son to the forest as he'd done before. By, the lad was fast… and he'd need to be, to get back here with help before—

Edward had heard what had happened in other villages round about. Of course he had. It was the talk of the region! How men dressed in black had decimated whole communities, snatching the inhabitants. No, not snatching; if you believed what was being said, they'd gone along willingly, whether they were alive or half dead. That made Edward shiver. The fact that not even death was enough for the likes of them, that you wouldn't even be able to rest then, but were called into the service of evil against your will.

The omens had been there, even if he hadn't heard about what had been happening. A darkening of the skies, the exact opposite of what you might expect at this time of year. But also a darkness that didn't go away, one that had *chased* away the sun, the light, causing the middle of the day to seem like dusk.

Only a matter of time, Edward supposed, before those troops showed up on their doorstep – and the next thing he knew they'd appeared on the outskirts of the village. Some on horseback, others on foot. Black against black.

Would Robin come to their aid, though? That was the question. He hadn't been able to do anything when those other settlements were attacked. Hadn't or couldn't… It had crossed Edward's mind, even as he'd sent Matthew on his way, that perhaps this scourge had already dealt with Hood and his men. It made sense to take out their biggest threat straight away so that nothing could stand against this blight.

At the moment, however, those newcomers were doing nothing. They'd been doing nothing for some time, had just gathered on the ridge overlooking their village and seemed to be waiting for something.

'What are they doing, Edward?' Alison asked him, pressing her head against his shoulder.

'I don't know, my love,' was the only reply he could offer her. Perhaps it was a way of torturing them, if the people of Wickham didn't actually know when the attack would come? But actually it was just buying them time; enough so that Matthew might return with Robin and the others, and then they'd stand a fighting chance hopefully. His friends and neighbours had stood shoulder-to-shoulder with the outlaws before, but they weren't really soldiers, didn't have the skills that Will Scarlet or Little John, or even Marion and Tuck had. They were simple folk who lived quiet lives for the most part, and weren't trained in combat. If it came to it, though, they'd defend their homes – their land – of that Edward was quite sure. They'd defend it with their lives.

'Do… do you think they'll come? Robin and the others?' his wife asked now, echoing his own thoughts.

'I…' Edward began, then broke into a smile before saying without doubt: 'Yes. Look!'

Alison followed his gaze, and his finger, to the edge of the woodland where they both saw their son emerge – followed soon after by Robin, Scarlet, Little John and Nasir. She frowned, waiting for more of them to come afterwards. When they didn't she said: 'Only four of them? But—'

'It'll be enough,' Edward told her. There was no denying that the full complement of Hood's men would have been preferable, but Edward had known as few as two or three of them take on many more men than this. 'At least they're here,' he reminded her, grateful for that alone. Their presence would give the others courage; it would *definitely* give them hope.

Keeping low, crouching down almost to Matthew's level, the men made their way across to the huts. They were all carrying bows and arrows, which would help should the troops in black decide to rush Wickham. Mathew made it over to them first and Alison took her son into her arms, delighted to see him again.

'Robin, Robin,' said Edward when the golden-haired leader of these people was close enough. 'I'm very glad to see you.'

Robin nodded. 'And it looks like we got here just in time. What's happening?'

'That's just it. *Nothing's* happening,' Edward informed him. 'They haven't moved an inch since they appeared up there. It's like they're waiting for something. A command to attack maybe?'

'A command from the Red Lord,' Robin said under his breath.

'Who?' It was the first time Edward had heard that particular name.

'Their leader,' said Little John. 'We've encountered him already… Well, Robin did anyway. *We* encountered some of his forces, almost didn't escape it.'

So, the soldiers did go after Robin and his band as Edward had thought. He was suddenly worried, though. 'Much, Tuck… Marion?'

'They're all right. That's to say Marion and Tuck are. Much is…' Robin paused as if he didn't know what to say next. '…he's unwell. Marion's tending to him and Tuck's keeping an eye out. He's also just got back from finding out what he could about all of this.' Which explained where the others were. Praise be to Herne they were still alive, thought Edward.

'What are they playin' at up there?' This was Scarlet, eyes narrowing as he watched the dark figures on the ridge.

'Let's find out,' said Robin. 'Nasir…?' He nodded for the Saracen to do what he did best, make his way up there and do a little reconnaissance.

And with that, Nasir was already gone.

'Is it me, or do they seem to be dressed differently?' said Little John.

Edward wouldn't know, he hadn't seen any of the others these men had fought. These particular soldiers, from what he could see, had chainmail on and helmets – similar to the outfits the Sheriff's men wore, but much more muted. They also boasted tunics with a symbol on them, a pair of wings that were... yes, were red in colour, Edward could see now. Obviously this Red Lord's insignia.

'Why are they just standin' there?' Scarlet again, impatient as ever – for them either to attack or for something to happen.

'Ready yourselves, just in case,' Robin said to them, and the rest of his people who were left took up positions where they had a clear line of sight with the bows and arrows. 'John, cover the rear. We've fallen for one of their traps before. We won't again.'

Little John nodded and went off to keep an eye on the back of the village.

And so, thought Edward, they were left to do what the men up there were doing. What they'd been doing since the intruders arrived.

They were all left to wait.

**

Likewise, all Marion could do was sit and wait while Robin and the others went off to help Edward, Alison and the rest of the villagers at Wickham. She got the impression Robin was quite glad she was remaining to keep an eye on Much. There hadn't really been any option, especially when they'd started discussing it and Much had reached out, grabbing her sleeve, her wrist, in a different way to before; desperate for her to remain there with him.

She was torn, though. On the one hand she wanted to be with Robin, John, Will and Nasir, but on the other Marion was the best qualified to attend to the young man. Though if Tuck was staying behind as well anyway...

Again, there had been no need to do that. It was almost as if Robin felt she needed protection, something they had argued about in the past. Hadn't Marion proved time and time again that she was more than capable of looking after herself? Robin had said it was because Tuck needed to rest, after his tour around information gathering, but there had been an unspoken request there when Robin looked at him. To make sure Tuck's 'Little Flower', as he called her, stayed safe.

There was always that inclination, to keep Marion out of harm's way – in spite of the fact Robin never seemed to understand it worked both ways. That she was just as worried about him when he was away from her side, like he was right now. But, ever since he visited Herne that seemed to have grown worse, like it was at the forefront of his mind. Not just keeping her safe either, it was as if he was frightened of losing all of this.

Did he not realise, that was on her mind all the time – simply because in the past she *had* lost it all? The man she loved, the friends she cared for more than she could possibly put into words. It was the main reason she'd tried to fight the affection she had for Robert. For *Robin*. That she railed against feelings that were becoming stronger by the day. And why shouldn't they? He was handsome, kind, brave (just look at the way he'd taken on the Red Lord single-handed), an excellent leader. Their leader. He'd taken on not only that name, Robin Hood, but the mantle of it as well. He'd earned the right to be called that, earned the right to wield Albion…

Earned the right to love her? For her to love him back?

Was Herne's chosen one becoming hers as well?

Marion shook the thoughts away; there were other things to worry about today. Not just Robin's wellbeing, how he was getting on in Wickham, but what was happening with Much. How he was growing sicker and sicker, and she could not determine a cause. Nor a cure.

Something about being in close contact with the Red Lord. Marion bit her lip as she thought about the stories Tuck had told, about the soulless, the damned. *Was* that to be Much's fate?

The monk – who was like a brother to her in more ways than one – had looked him over and was just as puzzled about what it could be. 'I think this might be beyond the realms of both of us,' he'd admitted, and then suggested they seek help from the horned protector of the forest. 'He might have an idea what to do next?'

But before they could talk about it any further, Tuck looked up and over the woodland. 'Wait… Listen, something's wrong.'

Even as he was getting up, leaning a bit too heavily on his stick and drawing his sword, Marion could feel it, could sense that something wasn't right in their makeshift camp, could sense the presence of evil. Then Tuck was crashing into the undergrowth, charging after whatever he thought was out there. 'Tuck! Tuck come back!' she called, grabbing her bow and priming it with an arrow.

Marion waited again; waited for movement out there. Moving slowly forwards to follow the ex-Friar, arrowhead swinging left and right. 'Tuck… Tuck are you all right? Where are you?'

No reply.

'Tuck? Why won't you—'

Marion heard the snapping of the twig behind her, realised there was someone there. Then she didn't have to wait any longer for anything.

Because there was a brief flash, pain. And as dark as the forest was, even in the middle of the day…

All she knew now was blackness.

CHAPTER 7

Nothing much had happened while Nasir had been gone, and Robin was beginning to wonder if it ever would – then caught himself, remembering you should be very careful not to tempt fate. Still, those soldiers up there had made no move towards Wickham and didn't look like they were going to anytime soon.

So, when Little John motioned that Nasir was skirting back around the village – and that he was not alone – Robin was at least thankful that something had occurred to break the monotony. 'He's… I think he's brought a prisoner with him,' said John, calling back and shrugging to them.

'A prisoner?' asked Scarlet.

'A prisoner,' Robin said when he saw Nasir pushing a man forwards, who had his hands bound behind his back.

'Aren't you going to introduce us to yer new friend?' Scarlet was looking the man up and down. He was indeed dressed very differently to the soldiers who'd attacked them all back in Sherwood, chainmail and tunic replacing that shiny black armour.

Nasir grimaced, the closest he ever got to smiling. He wrenched off the man's helmet, clicking his fingers up against the side of the man's head, but there was no reaction. 'Not Al-ghul. Alive, but…' Another click; the man didn't even seem to hear it. 'The others did not notice when I took him.'

'Possessed?' offered John, looking at Nasir and Scarlet in turn. In their time, all three had been in the same position. Robin had heard the story of how John had come to join the group in the first place, how he'd been captured by the Sorcerer Belleme's men and bewitched. How the other Robin had set him free… Nasir had been in the employ of that man, too, and owed a similar debt – but had also been placed under a spell by Gulnar back at Crom Cruac, mumbling words over and over in his mother tongue, his eyes as glazed over as the person's in front of them. While not exactly 'possessed' as such, Scarlet had been made to believe that his dead wife was returned to him – that they could live a normal life together. More of Gulnar's trickery, and something Scarlet still didn't like to talk about because it was too painful for him.

This man just looked…tormented. Robin didn't know how else to describe it. The person he'd been was still in there, behind those eyes; just suppressed, controlled. A puppet of a man, just in a different way to those others. A puppet created by—

The soldier turned his head suddenly, looked directly at Robin. Everyone tensed. Nasir's swords were immediately drawn, thinking he'd brought danger back with him. John's staff was raised and Scarlet's arrow was trained at the soldier's head: a shot that, point-blank, would kill him in an instant. Regardless of this, the man smiled a chilling smile. And when he spoke, Robin – who himself had Albion's tip at the fellow's throat – recognised the voice immediately. He'd last heard it bidding him farewell, though not goodbye, at the river's edge.

'Robin i' the Hood,' came the deep, rumbling timbre. 'I knew that you would come.'

'The Red Lord,' said Robin, half a question and half a gasp of amazement.

The bound man, the puppet, curled his lip. '*That* is not my name!'

'Lord Dragos then,' Robin conceded.

'Dragos?' snarled Scarlet. 'Let's kill 'im!'

'No, Will!' snapped Robin, swinging his sword and forcing Scarlet's arrow downwards before he could fire. 'Don't you understand? That's not really him. He's just using this man. There's still a chance he might recover, you'd be killing an innocent. One that Dragos picked up touring the villages.'

Scarlet scrunched up his face, but backed off, leaving Robin to resume his conversation. 'How are you… Can you see me?'

'I can see *everything*,' the man mouthed in a voice that was almost certainly not his own.

'No one can see everything,' Robin replied – and he thought back to what he'd told Herne, that nobody could live forever either. What if Dragos *could* see everything, including what would happen in the future, just like the spirit god of Sherwood could. What if the evil forces he served gave him that ability? Such an enemy might be unstoppable.

'As you wish,' was the reply.

'Why are you doing this?' asked Robin. 'For money? For the Sheriff's money?'

The man wearing Dragos' red wings on his chest laughed. 'Not any longer,' he said eventually. 'There is something I crave more than anything. A prize worth more than any gold.'

'A kingdom,' said Robin. 'Darkness never-ending, and your own kingdom. Here, on these shores.'

'In part, in part. That, and so much more.' Dragos, it seemed, spoke in riddles just like Herne. 'You seek to prevent me? Just as I sought you out when I came to the forest.'

'I must,' said Robin, hoping against hope he wasn't truly unstoppable.

'But you have a choice. You could walk away.' Robin was shaking his head even before Dragos was finished. 'Or even...'

'Even what?'

'Join me. Renounce the woodland deity. You and your men. I could offer them eternal life, and you... the commander of my forces.'

Robin couldn't believe what he was hearing, and judging from the expression on his friends' faces he wasn't the only one. 'Eternal life? Eternal suffering more like, with you as our master? Doesn't sound very appealing.'

The man chuckled. 'Oh, you have no idea the delights you deny yourself, little man. But it is your decision.'

'I *will* face you. I have to,' Robin told him. 'But first, I'll stop your men from taking Wickham.'

Another deep laugh. 'I have no interest in your pets here. Not yet anyway.'

'No interest...' Then Robin remembered something Dragos had said earlier, that he knew the Hooded Man would come. Of course he would. Wickham was being threatened when all was said and done. And the men up there, waiting. Not the ones in black armour, the black knights – the damned – but the 'possessed' as John had put it, the beguiled. All turning around now, even as the dialogue was drawing to a close. Turning and heading off in the direction they'd come from.

'I don't understand,' said Edward. 'Where are they going?'

'This was never about Wickham.' Robin grabbed hold of the man's tunic, forgetting what he'd said to Scarlet, that this wasn't really the Red Lord – it was the closest he'd get to him right now. 'Was it?'

More laughter, then the fellow slumped, letting Robin take the weight of his body, Dragos having left him for now. 'Edward, take him. Make sure you keep him securely tied, but don't let any harm come to him.'

'Robin?' asked his bearded friend, still not grasping what had happened. John, Scarlet and Nasir had, though.

'This was never about attacking your village, Edward,' Robin told him, already getting ready to leave again. 'It wasn't about killing your people or swelling the Red Lord's ranks. It was a distraction. Dragos was drawing us out of Sherwood. He wanted us here for a reason.'

'But why?' asked Edward, and for a second or two he looked as tormented as the man who'd been channelling the giant.

Robin didn't answer him, not just because he was rounding up his own troops, but because if he said it that would make it true. He knew what was back in Sherwood, three people that he cared about, that he couldn't bear to lose. But one in particular, that if she was lost to him would tear them all apart.

Marion, always Marion.

CHAPTER 8

Tuck felt like a complete and utter fool.

He'd been stumbling about in the undergrowth, had somehow got lost and ended up chasing his own tail, before making it back to camp. He could have sworn there had been something out there, something in the shadows – he'd heard, seen and, more than that, *felt* it. Those men in black armour coming back, perhaps? He'd wanted to head them off, not really thinking through what he might do if he came up against them. Anyway, by the time he managed to double back again, Marion was gone.

'Little Flower?' he called out then, because he was especially worried and felt especially guilty: 'Marion? Marion, where are you?'

Nothing. No sign of her and she wasn't answering his calls which, if he'd been thinking clearly, he'd have realised were giving away his position. Another shout and this time there *was* a response, in the form of figures appearing through the long grass. Tuck started, then recognised the friends who'd set off a few hours ago to help the people of Wickham.

'Tuck, we could hear you from the outskirts of Sherwood!' grumbled Scarlet.

Then they were all around him, asking what was wrong, although from their expressions it was clear they had a fair idea. That and the fact he'd been calling out a certain name.

'What happened?' asked Robin and Tuck explained as best he could, although even he had to admit it sounded odd when he started to put it into words. 'Another distraction,' their leader concluded.

'And where's Much?' This was John again, looking around. Tuck had been so concerned as to where Marion was, he hadn't noticed that the boy was missing from his position resting under the tree. Two of them now!

Nasir grunted to get their attention. 'One set of tracks,' he said, pointing with a dagger into the undergrowth. 'That way.'

'One set...' John rubbed at his beard. 'But—'

'Don't think,' said Robin, 'just go!' And with that they headed off to follow Nasir, Tuck struggling to keep up as they raced through the forest, just as he had when they were escaping the black knights that had invaded their home.

It seemed to him they were following those tracks even longer than he'd been on the road, trying to find out who or what was behind everything. What he'd discovered out there was an overwhelming sense of dread: people were scared and when they were scared they rarely hid it. Sometimes you had to take gossip and hearsay with a pinch of salt, but on this occasion the stories were so consistent it hadn't been that hard to build up a picture of what had transpired and what was *still* transpiring. One man he'd spoken to had a cousin who'd been present at one of the first attacks this so-called Red Lord had initiated.

'She said it was like the end of the world. Like demons were roaming the land!' he'd said, spittle flying from his mouth.

Not the end of the world, not yet. But if Robin was correct, then that was what this man... if you could call him a man... had in mind. The end of the world as they knew it at any rate, turning them all into pawns of one sort or another. With one person sat on the throne!

Tuck was puffing and sweating, had almost lost sight of the figures ahead of him, especially in the gloom that had descended on Sherwood of late. He only caught up, in fact, because they'd stopped. And they'd only stopped because they'd caught up with Much: the person who'd been making those tracks, who Tuck had last seen flat on his back, barely able to move. The lad's recovery was nothing short of miraculous, as if he'd had access again to the Cross of St Ciricus.

Robin, John and Scarlet were now surrounding Much, to prevent him from getting away if nothing else. Because every now and again he'd jerk forwards as if attempting to break free, as if he didn't realise who they all were, didn't know they were his friends.

By the time Tuck arrived, having to lean on Little John to get his breath back, the questioning was well underway.

'...made you do that? Much? Much, can you hear me?'

'...why were you...?'

'...can't you tell us...?'

All of them, speaking over each other to the point where Tuck was getting confused himself, let alone Much. 'What's going on?' he asked John. 'What happened?'

John leaned in. 'We got here in time to see Much handing Marion over to some riders in black armour. The Red Lord's personal guard.' Tuck thought the large man was going to spit at the ground then, and he wouldn't have blamed him. 'Nasir tried to catch up with them, but they got away. He's off trying to track them right now.'

'Much...? I don't believe it.'

'I doubt I would if I hadn't seen it with my own two eyes. But look at him, he doesn't know where or who he is.' John was right about that, Much was gazing about him like he was seeing something the rest of them couldn't, cocking his head as if hearing things. 'We saw someone just like him back at Wickham,' John concluded.

Was this the end result of whatever had struck Much down? thought Tuck. Had he ended up as one of the Red Lord's slaves after all? Tuck just had to hope it was temporary, whatever it was.

The lad made another bid to get away and this time Scarlet grabbed him, trying to hold him in spite of the squirming about he was doing. Much promptly ducked his head and bit Scarlet on the arm.

'Oww!' he shouted, letting Much go. 'Why, you...'

Much shot off in the other direction, but wasn't running. Instead, he was scrambling around almost on all fours.

'He's like a wild animal!' gasped John.

'I'll give 'im wild!' was Scarlet's response.

Robin stood in his way this time and Much clambered up him, attempting to claw at his face. The blond man got hold of him by the wrists, but had to jerk his own head back to prevent Much snapping at his face, perhaps even biting his nose off. In the end he was forced to let go.

'Gone mad, 'e has!' Again this was Scarlet, still clutching at his arm.

John was the next to tackle him, but Much managed to crawl through his legs. It was like one of those games they often played in Sherwood to stave off boredom, thought Tuck: tug of war, or blind man's buff. Only this one wasn't fun, no fun at all! The expression on Much's face was one of pure hatred, a wounded creature lashing out because it didn't want to be caught... or put down.

'Right,' Tuck said to himself. 'That's quite enough of that.' He barrelled into Much from the side, sending him spinning and crashing to the ground. Then, when he was down there, wondering what had hit him, Tuck sat on the lad to keep him still. He looked up at the others. 'What are you waiting for? Restrain him! I'm not going to sit here all day.' John went to find some vines, but Much kept bucking and trying to throw Tuck off. 'Hurry, he's getting stronger by the moment. I'm not sure how much longer I can—'

It was at that moment Scarlet appeared at the side of him, bent down, and punched Much in the face. He stopped struggling immediately. 'Now 'e's restrained.'

'The softly, softly approach as always,' said Tuck holding out his hand for Robin to pull him up – though it took both him and Scarlet to eventually do so.

'Worked, didn't it?' was Scarlet's reply, and he went back to rubbing his arm.

'So, what now?' asked John as he returned with the vines and began to secure Much's wrists.

Tuck thought about what he'd said to Marion about Much before he'd left camp, before he'd left *her*, with the daft notion of trying to protect the woman at the forefront of his mind; that silent look between himself and Robin a promise that he would. A promise he'd broken. 'We need help,' he said.

'Oh, you *reckon*, do ya?'

'Be quiet, Will,' said Robin.

'As I was saying,' Tuck carried on. 'We need to get him to Herne. He'll know what to do.' It would take a supernatural being to cure a supernatural affliction.

Robin nodded, understanding the wisdom of Tuck's words. But he was also looking back towards the edge of Sherwood, to where Tuck assumed Marion had been taken. 'Don't worry,' the monk said to him, placing a hand on his arm. 'Don't worry, Nasir is following them. We'll get her back.'

'I hope so. I really do.'

Their leader met Tuck's eyes then, another silent look, and the sadness in them was so overwhelming the ex-Friar had to turn away first because he felt guilty, because he felt like such a fool.

And because he hoped, rather than knew for sure, there was some truth to his own words.

CHAPTER 9

Once again, the great hall echoed with the sound of unannounced footfalls.

This time, it was a surprise visit from someone he knew marginally better than the last 'unexpected' visitor they'd received here. Robert de Rainault, the Sheriff of Nottingham, watched as his sibling Abbot Hugo swept into the room – looking for all the world like he was floating under that huge purple cassock he always wore. The hat he had on, which covered his ears, and the gold jewellery – on display now he'd shrugged off his cloak – completed the image.

'Brother!' said the Sheriff, 'this is an unexpected delight.' His tone, as always, said exactly the opposite. He was already in a bad mood, due in no small part to Gisburne's gibberings, which had been going on for some time. He'd been delivering reports about what was happening outside of the castle walls, in the neighbouring boroughs, villages and even further afield. The Sheriff liked to keep abreast of what was going on, especially where taxes and money were concerned. But the topic this time seemed to be the exploits of the person he'd hired to get rid of Robin Hood. It still boiled his blood to think of him as Robert of Huntingdon and the betrayal which had accompanied that revelation.

The Sheriff was used to the peasants being in panic about something or other, it helped keep them in line. He wasn't averse to culling the population a little either when needs must, usually as part of some scheme or other. And he'd been privy to Lord Dragos' own plans in advance – he wouldn't have signed off on those payments if he hadn't, with assurances naturally that this man could get the job done. According to him, Hood and his outlaws were in a state of disarray, running scared after Dragos and his men had ventured into the forest at night-time. A bold move indeed, and something the Sheriff would never have considered in a million years. It would be suicide!.

'That,' Dragos had said, 'is where you and I disagree.'

Disrupting Hood's network of villages in league with him was only the next step. And, it had to be said, there had been no reports of robberies or bandits since that mercenary appeared. So the Sheriff had been happy to hand over a certain amount of money to the man… Perhaps happy was not the right word. The Sheriff had been unable to see any reason why he *shouldn't* pay him, which, he had to admit, wasn't his usual position. Something about Dragos' eyes, the way he looked at him…

In any event, what he'd been less happy about was the state of Nottingham market, how there had been fewer traders than usual. 'There have to be the men to farm,' Gisburne had been explaining as part of his account. 'To take the food to the market to sell.'

'You're teaching me, the Sheriff of Nottingham, about how commerce works?' He'd almost laughed in the man's face.

'No, of course not my lord. It's just that—'

'You really are the most tedious cretin. Sometimes I really don't know why I keep you around.'

'My lord,' argued Gisburne, 'it's because of the Red L—'

'How many times have I told you not to call him by that name, Gisburne!' He could feel his right eye narrowing at that point, as it had a tendency to do when he was provoked. 'He almost killed you for it the last time. Perhaps I should have let him!'

'My apologies. Lord Dragos,' the blond man said under duress. 'It is because of his interference that profits from the villages are down. All of which affects the amount of money they can pay in taxes.'

'You're seriously taking their side, the people?' The Sheriff had tutted.

'No, that's not what I'm saying at all, it's just that—'

'I know exactly what I'm doing, Gisburne! Credit me with some sense, will you?' His aide had looked at him in that way he did sometimes, which said that he didn't credit the Sheriff with any sense at all. The kind of look that made him want to string 'Sir' Guy up, or put him in the stocks for a fortnight to teach *him* a lesson or two. It wasn't that he couldn't see Gisburne's point; *of course* he knew that without farmers there were no crops, and without crops there was no money for taxes. In that respect perhaps Lord Dragos had been a tad… heavy-handed. It was just that what had been set in motion had to be played out, the plan followed through. Once this was all over, they'd reap the rewards of free passage through Sherwood, then the rich, the titled and, yes, even Royalty, would grace Nottingham with their presence on a more frequent basis. That would make up for any number of poor market days. Sometimes sacrifice was necessary in order to progress, but he didn't expect Gisburne to understand that. Besides, he could always use the man as a scapegoat if anything went wrong. The thought had crossed his mind in the past, and would probably do so again should the need arise in the future.

Like now, for instance, as his brother the Abbot approached, face as grim as ever. He was a schemer just like the Sheriff, this one – the church a fit place for someone with a mind as devious as his. However their other sibling Edward, who had died in the Crusades, had been born so virtuous was anyone's guess. He had certainly been the odd one out in their family.

A small messenger, out of breath, finally entered some distance behind the holy man and began to announce him. 'My Lord, the Abbot Hu…' The Sheriff fixed the tiny man with a glare that would curdle milk, as he tried to think of a fitting punishment for later on. 'Abbot Hugo,' he finished, voice tailing off in fear. At least he *had* announced this visitor – albeit late – which was more than he'd done when Lord Dragos had wandered into the great chamber. They'd discovered the diminutive imbecile some time later, simply gazing at the walls of the castle. Perhaps the Sheriff would put him in the dungeons where he'd be able to gaze at them to his heart's content?

'Get out!' he barked, but the messenger was already on his way. Would be on his way out through the castle gates if he had any sense. 'Now then, brother, where was I? Oh yes, what brings you to Nottingham this fine day?'

'Fine day?' Hugo grumbled. 'Clearly you haven't ventured outside in a while, Robert. Fine days are but a memory of late.'

The Sheriff had noticed the terrible weather recently, but he'd had other matters on his mind. Besides, this was England: the weather was always terrible. 'I'm quite sure you didn't come all this way just to discuss the climate, brother dear. Though Heaven knows, these people are more than happy to talk about that till doomsday.'

'Ah, it's funny you should mention that particular day,' the Abbot said, sneering, though he didn't say why.

'So, what *are* you doing here?' asked the Sheriff, finally.

'I came to see if the rumours were true.'

'Rumours? What rumours?'

'Oh, come along, Robert! Don't play games with me. That didn't even work when we were children.' The Abbot wagged his finger in his brother's direction for emphasis.

'No,' admitted the Sheriff, leaning back on his chair… his throne, 'it didn't, did it.'

Hugo joined them both at the front, more footfalls echoing throughout the hall. 'Tell me, these tales about missing villagers I've been hearing... Are they connected to the fact that you recently hired a mercenary from the east?'

'They... they might be,' the Sheriff was forced to admit. He'd never been very good at lying to Hugo, especially when the man was only a few feet away. 'What of it?'

'And is it true that said mercenary is one Dragos the Red?' Hugo waited, but when the Sheriff didn't reply he said: 'I'll take that as a yes. Robert, have you *completely* lost your mind?'

'I...'

'Men falling into a stupor, then going off with him. This is what he does!' Hugo banged his fist on a table not far away. 'This is how he came by his power abroad, how he maintained it. Have you not heard about the dark methods he employs? That those recruits to his cause will fight to the death for him, and not even feel it when they're wounded? My God, Robert – it was only because of the holy men in his homeland that they were able to chase him away in the first place!'

'No, no I hadn't heard about all that.' The Sheriff turned his head and faced his second-in-command. 'You left those little details out of your story, Gisburne.'

'I did try to tell you that he—'

The Sheriff waved his hand to silence Gisburne, and regarded his brother once more. 'As far as I was aware... All that I was concerned about, that interested me, was his fearsome reputation as a fighter.'

'Then why did you not find out more?' Hugo sighed. 'A maniac loose on these shores, and *you* brought him here! All because of your ongoing feud with Robin Hood. It has blinded you once again!'

'Ah, now... We haven't had any trouble from Hood and his people since we hired Dragos,' countered the Sheriff.

'But he's not dead,' said the Abbot. It wasn't really a question.

'No, not yet. But soon, I'm promised. He's running scared and those who give him aid are decimated.'

'These would be the people you also rely on for your taxes, would it not?' It was the same thing Gisburne had been wittering on about.

'Yes, but in time—'

'Time? We're running out of time, brother!' Hugo was pointing again, his finger as deadly as any crossbow bolt. 'Don't you see, the outlaws, those who assist him... None of that matters! You'll soon have a bigger problem than

Robin Hood to worry about. Now this man has his feet under the table, now that he's begun his work over here, he could build an army bigger than yours. Bigger even than the King's! And if I've heard about this, how long do you think it will take for word to reach our esteemed ruler?'

The Sheriff slumped down further into his chair. He could feel all the blood draining from his face; probably looked paler even than Dragos himself at that moment. The King: that was the last thing he needed…another visit from *him*! The previous one hadn't exactly gone well, culminating with Marion escaping from his chambers. If it hadn't been for the fact he was trying to make the people believe he was a benevolent and kindly ruler at present, they'd all have been for it!

'Do we know where the Red Lord is right now, Gisburne?' Hugo asked.

The Sheriff didn't correct his brother when he used that name and couldn't help noticing a slight smirk from Gisburne. 'There is talk he has taken up residence at an abandoned castle on the coast. Probably used the money the Sheriff paid him in advance to buy the land and fortify it.'

Something else the Sheriff hadn't been informed about. Instead of telling him things he already knew, like how trade worked, why hadn't Gisburne been furnishing him with facts like these? What a traitorous snake he really was, thought the Sheriff… not that *he* could talk.

'A *castle!*' Hugo shook his head in despair, and began jabbing that finger at his brother once more. 'You'd better think of something to get that man in line. And quickly, before this all spirals out of control!'

Then he turned, barking at the servants to prepare his chambers. The great hall echoed again with the sound of his footfalls, exiting this time.

'So, what now?' asked Gisburne, as if nothing had happened. As if he was still the Sheriff's best friend, instead of playing people off against each other. When he didn't get his answer, Gisburne asked the question again.

'Oh, be silent, will you!' the Sheriff snapped back, all patience with the man gone. 'I'm thinking.' But of course, he always had a plan – *plans* plural more often than not. Schemes to match his brother's and Dragos' plotting, three or four steps ahead of Gisburne certainly.

He suddenly felt a smile breaking on his face. Yes, it was so perfect. Brilliant, in fact! If he played it just right, this was one game he was destined to win outright. And for all their sakes, he hoped Robin Hood *wasn't* dead yet and that Dragos hadn't finished him off.

Because he would have use of him soon enough.

CHAPTER 10

As they made their way through Sherwood, towards that clearing he knew so well – that he was called to, *pulled* to occasionally, where all this had begun – Robin felt a different kind of pull. And he wondered if he was doing the right thing.

Tuck had spotted him looking over his shoulder, both back at the camp and constantly on the journey. Worried about Marion, wondering if she was all right. Wanting to just go back off in the other direction, catch up with Nasir and find out where they'd taken her, so they could go after her.

Robin had been stupid to leave her side in the first place, but had thought she was safe enough back here with the monk and with Much… Little realising it was the miller's son they'd had to worry about the most. Who would deliver her to the Red Lord's men. She'd have been better off in Wickham with the rest of them.

He glanced over at the unconscious form of Much, being carried on Little John's shoulder this time as if he was light as a feather – this, regardless of John joking about him weighing a ton, that it was all the venison. No-one had laughed, though; it had just reminded them of how content they'd been after that meal, just before—

All except Robin, of course. He hadn't been able to settle even back then, worrying about what might go wrong, about what Herne had said that he'd lose. Strangely, now he knew for sure it was Marion – and it still might not *just* be Marion – he wanted to get on with things: act, fight, whatever. Do something!

You *are* doing something, he reminded himself: you're trying to help your friend. 'Careful,' he'd said as John was loading the young man up; a mirror of what they'd seen when Much was carrying an unconscious Marion, when he'd simply handed her over to those armoured men. Laying her on the back of one of the horses.

'Careful!' Scarlet had ranted. '*Careful?* Where was careful when 'e bit my arm?'

'He didn't know what he was doing,' Robin insisted yet again. When… if Much woke up out of this, he'd be as horrified as anyone at his actions.

But Scarlet hadn't been listening. As he'd been doing all the way here, he was still examining that bite on his forearm, convinced he himself would come down with the same affliction.

'I don't think it works that way,' Tuck had assured him and Robin agreed, still hoping he'd come back to them and that he wouldn't be someone else they'd lose… Robin pushed the thought away which followed: that there might be even more losses to come.

Maybe Herne might be able to tell him more, might clarify some of the things he'd told him originally. Another hope. But first, Much.

They needed his help with Much.

***

Much was starting to stir.

Feeling the call, the pull. The same one he'd felt since he found himself on that dirt track with that man who… who wasn't an ordinary man at all. He understood that not long afterwards, understood exactly what his lord, his master could do. What he wanted to achieve. The peace he could bring to this country, perhaps even the world one day.

He'd fought it at first, oh how he'd fought it! Much knew he wasn't the strongest of their band, but he didn't give up easily. Yet he kept seeing those eyes – the eyes back there on the dirt track. He saw them in his dreams, in nightmares, after he'd grown too weary to walk anymore. Saw the flapping of great wings, of something dark. Of many somethings. Somehow he was aware of shouting out in his sleep, that he might be disturbing the others, but he couldn't help it. He saw what he saw. Heard that voice, the one which called out to him and said:

'*You belong to me now!*'

Much tried not to listen, but it was insistent and it made promises. Promises about how he could live forever, that he wouldn't suffer the same fate as the first Robin who'd looked after him all that time; his foster brother. Who'd promised on that hill, surrounded by the Sheriff's men, that he'd join Much later. That he'd stay alive… Only for Marion to convince Much – asking why Robin would give her Albion – that he was truly gone.

He remembered how let down he'd felt by that, even though deep inside he knew Robin hadn't wanted to leave him, leave any of them. Leave Marion. Then a spark of hope, when they'd heard a hooded man had released John, Will, Tuck, Nasir and Edward. A spark that became a flame of hope when they saw that burning arrow rise and fall into the water to join theirown.

But that mysterious hooded man had walked off and left them. Left them for a whole year, left them divided, scattered. Much had cried a lot during that time, but realised there was no sense in it. He was a shepherd, the same as Little John, and that was that. Time to grow up. Not the miller's son anymore. Not anyone's son…

Then Robert of Huntingdon had come along, trying to tell them it had been him, that *he* was Herne's son and was now Robin Hood. That, if they were willing, he wanted to start it all up again, which he had succeeded in doing. But wasn't there a part of Much that resented the Earl's son for walking away in the first place? For not coming back and joining them?

'*He let you down,*' said the voice. '*I won't. Join me.*'

No, no! He loved this Robin – they all did. He'd done his best to make up for everything, to look after Much.

'*He let you down,*' the voice repeated. '*He let you down.*'

In the end he hadn't been able to hold out, he'd let the voice of his new master in. Felt compelled to obey it. And once that had happened, he belonged to the figure with the red armour and the eyes… *those eyes!*

'What… what do you want from me?' Much had asked and his lord had told him. That they thought he was sick – far from it – and that when the others left, he should make sure Marion didn't. That Much had to make sure the woman stayed with him, to tend him.

Neither of them had been expecting Tuck to remain as well, but Much's master had used that same dark magic to draw him into the forest – making *him* think he was hearing things, feeling things, and then causing him to lose his way…

And while he was absent, Much had a task to complete. '*Bring her to the edge of the trees. My men will be waiting.*'

Even as he'd knocked her out with a nearby log, he'd wondered if it was the right thing to do, had mouthed words of contrition. He'd had tears in his eyes then as well. But it had to be done, his lord had chosen. Much had felt the pull, carrying Marion on his shoulder and taking her to meet with those armoured riders: delivering her.

It had been pure instinct after that, but not his own. Not a man's instinct: a trapped animal's. He couldn't let the others get near him, take him.

'They will kill you for what you have done,' the voice said.

He didn't want to die. He wanted to live forever. And so again he'd fought, even though he knew it was wrong, that those people were his friends. Robin, Will… he'd bitten Will! John, Tuck, who'd flattened him and pinned him to the ground.

Then blackness again, a blow. And the nightmares, of redness and eyes. Until he was drawing near to somewhere, a place they were taking him. A place the voice didn't want him to be.

'They're trying to take you away from me,' it said. *'Don't let them, Much. Fight again. Fight them!'*

That's when he'd begun to stir, to realise he was being carried himself over Little John's strong shoulder.

That's when he'd started to wriggle, to kick out, to force the big man to drop him. His hands were tied together, but he'd soon fix that. Bite through them with his teeth or even… Yes, grab a knife. Robin's knife, the one he always kept on his belt.

It had all happened so quickly, they didn't have time to stop him.

And he didn't have time to make them understand, he was just obeying his lord. Obeying the pull…

The call.

***

'What did you go an' let 'im do that for?'

Robin threw Scarlet a filthy look. It hadn't exactly been a case of *letting* him do anything. Much had got free of John and snatched the knife before Robin could stop him, and now the lad – still bound at the wrists – had a weapon… aside from those snapping teeth of his.

'Watch out!' warned John, as Much swung the knife in Tuck's direction and only missed him by a whisker.

'Praise be!' said the monk who'd narrowly avoided the blade, crossing himself.

'Much! Much, it's us! Try to think!' shouted Robin.

'Not easy for 'im at the best of times!' snarled Scarlet in frustration.

Something else was happening, though. While they'd been concentrating on Much – the flashing knife – a strange mist had started rolling in, covering the floor of the forest. Then a light, all the brighter because of the dimness inside Sherwood and the sky above it.

'What *is* that?' asked John when he finally noticed it.

The source was revealed soon enough: a flame. A torch. And a figure following behind, towering above them all, those antlers curling up and up, the fur reaching down – lost in that supernatural swirl of fog.

'Herne,' breathed Robin, and he couldn't help smiling in spite of everything that had gone wrong for them – that was *still* going wrong.

Much turned and for a moment was as in awe as the rest of them, which happened whenever they were in the presence of this forest spirit. The next thing they knew, the lad was snarling again, rushing towards Herne, this time with the knife out. The figure barely twitched, watched Much's approach with interest, but the expression on his face did not change at all. He simply lowered the torch when the young man was near enough, burning his hands and causing him to drop the weapon.

The lad looked up and it was only now that an expression of pure terror crossed his face.

'Hold him!' boomed Herne's voice, and Little John and Scarlet did as they were told, regardless of the struggling. Herne pulled up Much's sleeve and then ran the flame along the skin. There was a howl, which might have been from the burning or something else and Much's eyes rolled back into his head. His body went slack and now the pair of them were holding him up or he'd have collapsed on the ground in a heap.

'Only the light,' said Herne, 'can defeat the darkness. Drive it out.'

'Fire,' said Tuck in hushed tones. 'Told you.'

'Is… is he going to be all right?' asked Robin, stepping forwards.

Herne handed him the torch. 'In time. Bring him,' he said to Robin, motioning for the men to carry Much into his domain. 'I would speak with you.' He turned and started walking off again into the mist.

Robin nodded at Scarlet and John, who handed Much over. Like a puppet whose strings had been cut, thought Robin as he dragged him along with his free hand.

Following his own lord, following the call.

***

Much was aware of what had happened.

The link was gone, the voice telling him what to do as well. He was aware he'd almost hurt his friends again, of the damage he had done. There was no-one feeding the feelings of resentment anymore, no matter how unfair they were.

No lord, no master whispering in his ear. Only another summons entirely, to listen to the Horned God of Sherwood, to begin healing so that he would be free of the evil. He was aware of Robin half-carrying, half-dragging him to Herne's cave – it felt like a dream again, but Much knew it was real. That they'd saved him at last. Which was more than they'd been able to do for Marion...

Oh no, Marion! he thought. He'd given her over to those men. What had he done? The wrong thing, definitely. Would she be all right?

Much hadn't been able to control his own actions so it hadn't really been his fault, and although it made no sense, he thought this: That as much as Robin might have let them down in their time of need, he'd done far worse. He'd let Robin down, let Marion down, let *all of them* down.

Much just hoped there was still time, that he'd have a chance to make up for it.

CHAPTER 11

Marion's eyes fluttered open.

She'd had the strangest dream… There had been a fight in Sherwood, against a huge man dressed in red armour and his followers

The Red Lord, yes that was it, who had been causing havoc out there in the villages. 'Recruiting' people.

Wickham… Yes, that's right, Wickham had been in danger and Robin had gone off to help. She'd remained behind with Much, because he'd been ill ever since the fight. And Tuck, but then he'd wandered off…

Pain. She remembered the pain, someone striking her from behind. She reached around to the back of her head and felt there, wincing at the lump that had formed while she'd been asleep, unconscious. But who'd done that to her, and where was she now?

Tentatively, she lifted her head and everything spun. Marion waited a second or two, then pushed herself upright, taking in her surroundings. She was lying on a bed, a huge bed had been grand at some point in the past but was now faded and worn. The sheets she lay on were fresh, however, so she'd been expected wherever she'd ended up. Had someone found her, rescued her from whoever had struck her back there in Sherwood? Brought her here… wherever here was? Not Nottingham castle, that much was certain. Not any that she recognised, though admittedly this was just one room.

It was very dim in there, just a few candles throwing out light – the window covered with shutters. There were cobwebs everywhere, hanging off chairs, the table opposite, which told her the place had been neglected for some time. There was no sign of her weapons: her bow and arrows, her sword. Marion swung her legs over the side of the bed and tried to stand, wobbling slightly as she did so and had to lean on one of the bed's posts for support.

You can do this, she told herself, gritting her teeth, and she pushed off, tottering towards the window. Marion practically slammed into the wall, taking deep breaths and praying she wouldn't just collapse right there on the spot. What she wouldn't give to be back in Sherwood now. She always felt better there, almost as if the place had healing properties of its own.

Moving sideways, she pulled back one of the wooden shutters on the arched window. It barely let any light in at all, and for a moment she thought it might be night, but then realised that these days there was little difference between night and day: it always dark out there. Another thing they had to thank the Red Lord for.

There were also thick iron bars on the window to stop anyone from escaping. To stop *her* from escaping. If she hadn't had a bad feeling about all this before, she definitely did now. This was a prisoner's room... or it had been turned into one, because why have a bed as ornate as that in it? Unless it was meant to keep someone of noble blood captive?

Marion swallowed dryly, looked over her shoulder and wished that she hadn't. The room was spinning now. But she had to get to the door, get out of here. Everything was telling her she was in danger, so much danger. She turned and staggered towards the huge barrier, which itself was riddled with woodworm judging from the holes; rotten, like everything else in this room, in this place. She could feel it, taste it on the air.

Grateful she'd made it across the room without passing out, she grabbed on to the handle of the door, turning it. She'd fully expected it to be locked, so was surprised when it clunked open and she was able to tug on it, pulling the wood towards her.

Stepping out, a breath caught in the back of her throat. On either side of the door, men had been posted. The men in black armour from the forest, the ones Nasir had called Al-ghul: men who were alive, but...empty...except for whatever darkness was inside them. Doomed. They stood stock still, as if they hadn't even noticed she was there, or had just opened the door. Marion remained still as well, in case it broke the spell.

Now she knew where she was. Not exactly where, but she knew who this castle must belong to. No amount of silly tricks, of made-up games like 'Conquest' that she'd played in the King's bedchambers at Nottingham, would help her now. No amount of shin-kicking.

Marion had to get out of there.

Determined, she suddenly took another step, making for the hallway beyond that room. Two swords were drawn in seconds, crossing in front of her, and she let out a shocked cry of surprise. So they did know she was there, after all. *Of course* they did… wouldn't be very effective guards if they didn't. And there was no way she was getting past them, either. Even if she was at full strength, tackling one would have been a challenge – let alone two!

Reluctantly, Marion backed away and almost as a reflex action the crossed swords were lowered once more, leaving that gap tantalisingly open again. She thought about making another break for it, but the same thing would happen – only this time she might not be so lucky and could even be injured in the attempt.

Sighing, she closed the door on them, mostly because she wanted to try and forget they were there. As she made her way back to the bed, realising she'd been upright for far too long and needed, rather than wanted, to lay down, she decided to pretend she *was* back home in the forest. That none of this had happened, that it had all just been a continuation of her bad dream

But as she stretched out, head back on the pillows, Marion bit her lip. And as she closed her eyes again, hoping for better dreams, she couldn't help thinking the nightmare, the *real* nightmare in the waking world…

Well, that was yet to come.

CHAPTER 12

They sat around a crackling fire, on a different day, a different night.

Not that long ago, they'd been feasting on the king's finest venison here. Now they didn't want to eat at all. Apart from Tuck, who was always hungry but knew better than to say anything at the moment, they'd all lost their appetites.

'I'm sick of all this hangin' around, we should be doing somethin'!' said Scarlet, suddenly getting up and grabbing his sword.

'Don't you think I *want* to?' Robin rose as well and faced him. 'But what can we do? Herne said to wait!'

It was true. The last time he'd spoken with the spirit, back when he'd taken Much to the cave, which seemed like so long ago now, his advice had been much clearer, even if Robin wished that it hadn't.

After laying the lad on a flat bit of rock, Robin had approached Herne. He'd seen this even before it had happened. And now Robin understood the prophecy: he needed to stop the man in red and his followers. But how could you stop men who didn't even feel pain, or weren't allowed to? Who were so great in number?

'And soon to be greater,' Herne informed him as if reading his thoughts. 'He continues to build his army.'

'Then how...?' Robin looked down. There were only six of them, five now they didn't have Much or Marion.

'We wait. Fear not, Robin. Marion is strong – and soon you will receive help from the most unexpected of sources.' Herne placed his hand on Robin's shoulder. 'Then, and only then, will you be able to truly sever the link between the Red Lord and those he has tainted, cutting the head off the snake. Have faith.'

'Faith?' Scarlet said now, as Robin reminded him of the advice. 'That lunatic's out there doing who knows what, getting stronger, adding more people to 'is ranks, and we're just sittin' here talkin' about faith!'

'Herne said we would get help. I have to trust that.'

'What kind of 'elp? Because right now I'd settle for an army!' Scarlet told his leader. 'But...' He looked around them, mocking. 'I don't see one anywhere lying around, do you?'

'Herne hasn't steered us wrong yet,' Little John pointed out to his friend.

'It's bad enough Much is still back there, John, still recoverin',' spat Scarlet. 'But Marion...'

'I *know!*' shouted Robin, cutting in, then lowered his voice. 'I know.'

'Poor Little Flower,' Tuck mumbled under his breath, which didn't help matters.

'We can stop this from gettin' any worse, that's what you said!' Scarlet reminded Robin.

He shook his head and sighed. 'It's not as if we even know where he's taken her,' Robin said eventually, remembering when he came back from the cave to find Nasir had returned. To hear that he'd lost the trail of the men on horseback, that according to him they'd simply disappeared. 'Where would we even start?'

'What are you lookin' at me for? I dunno!' It was Scarlet's turn to shake his head. 'Somewhere... *anywhere!*'

'I know, but we can't just—' Robin was interrupted by a noise, someone approaching. If he'd wanted to, this man could have crept up on them and nobody would have known about it, but he intended them to hear him. And this time Nasir had, if not better news than the last time when he'd lost those men, *more surprising* news.

'Nas,' said Little John. 'What is it?'

'The Sheriff and a handful his men,' replied the Saracen. 'On the outskirts of the forest. He says he has a proposition for you, Robin.'

They looked at each other then, all equally puzzled.

***

They'd warned him not to go, probably remembering the farce that had happened last time, when the Sheriff had double-crossed him during the exchange of Martin for Much. If it hadn't been for Adam Bell having a change of heart, Robin would be dead instead of that old bandit.

'It's a trick,' John had said.

'A trap!' Scarlet concurred.

But he had to see what the Sheriff wanted. To come to the edge of Sherwood personally and ask to see Robin, that meant only two things: he wanted something from him, and he was desperate.

'Just be careful,' Tuck had warned and he'd nodded. The man was still feeling guilty about Marion, he knew. But then, weren't they all?

Robin had broken cover with his bow primed, arrow pointing at the Sheriff who was on horseback. Gisburne, his lackey, was mounted next to him. More arrows were trained on that man and the escort riders, and at the first sign of trouble those projectiles would find their marks. But the Sheriff would have assumed that was the case. There'd be no need to spell it out.

When he was close enough, Robin called over: 'What do you want, Sheriff?'

'You'll speak when you're spoken to, wolfshead!' snapped Gisburne. Ever the double-act, him and his master.

The Sheriff waved a hand to silence his lapdog. 'I have a proposal for you.'

Robin almost laughed out loud. 'A proposal?'

'You heard him!' bellowed Gisburne, which earned him a sideways look this time.

When the Sheriff, bobbing up and down on his horse, turned back to Robin, he said: 'Yes. I believe we have a common enemy.'

'Oh?' replied Robin. 'And who might that be?'

'Lord Dragos... The Red Lord.' This drew a look from Gisburne, as if he shouldn't be referring to the man in this fashion, as if he'd been told not to himself. But that was always the Sheriff's way: do as he said, and not what he did.

'Really? And here was I thinking that you *summoned* him? That everything that's happened is all down to you, all your fault!' Robin was tempted to just put an arrow in the man anyway, retaliation for what he'd done. There would probably never be a better opportunity, but in spite of this he held himself in check.

The Sheriff smirked. 'I did. But... how can I put this, the Red Lord has overstepped the mark.'

'He's out of your control, you mean,' snapped Robin. 'If he was ever under it in the first place.'

The smirk turned into a sneer.

'Admit it! You made a mistake, Sheriff.'

'I... I made an error in judgment, trusted the wrong person. Thought he was someone he turned out not to be. And not for the first time, Robin... Or should I say Robert?' The Sheriff's words were full of sadness but also resentment.

'Robin will do just fine,' he told him.

'So… do you want to hear what I've got to say or not?'

He paused for a moment, before speaking again. 'Tell me,' said Robin, then listened to his arch enemy's plans.

***

'What's goin' on?' asked Scarlet, keeping the string on his bow taut. 'Why's he takin' so long?'

'Probably just catching up,' suggested John.

'It's takin' too long,' Scarlet said, who had Gisburne in his sights and was just looking for an excuse to kill the man, especially after he'd dragged him to the top of that rock blindfolded and bound during that St Ciricus debacle. He'd have finished him there and then if it hadn't been for Robin.

'It'll take as long as it takes,' Tuck told him. 'Let them talk.'

Eventually, the Sheriff and his men turned around and began riding off in the opposite direction to the forest. Robin, now lowering his bow, jogged back to join his friends.

'Well?' asked Scarlet, putting his own bow down as Robin returned. '*Well?* What did 'e want?'

Robin just smiled. 'You should be happy, Will,' he said.

'What? 'appy?' He turned to John. 'What's 'e talkin' about?'

'I'm sure he'll tell you, if you give him a chance,' Tuck admonished.

'You should be happy because… I've just found you your army,' Robin told him. Then he smiled again at the confusion on Scarlet's face.

CHAPTER 13

It wasn't the first time Marion had been held captive. Far from it.

But it was the first time she'd been made to wait so long before being taken to her captor. In this case, that wasn't such a bad thing. She'd gladly have waited centuries to meet the Red Lord again – not that she'd actually met him the last time, so much as fought him, fled from him.

There was no fleeing now, however. No escaping the guards at her door, who'd periodically left her meagre rations of bread and water to live on, but had now flung that door wide open and were pulling her from the bed as she kicked and shouted. They took no notice, had one job to do and were focused totally on that: dragging her down the stairs to a lower level.

'Where are you taking me?' she asked them, but in her heart of hearts wasn't really expecting an answer. These cursed people were incapable now of thinking for themselves; there was nothing of them left inside.

She remembered years ago, being dragged down a corridor like the one she was in now. The Baron de Belleme hadn't made her wait, more's the pity. He'd been in a particular hurry to sacrifice her as she hung from a pentangle. Then there was Owen of Clun, who'd stolen Marion away from her father's side and ordered Gulnar to give her a potion to make her more... pliable. Black magic once again. Different times, different Robins rushing to her aid, but similar situations. History repeated itself again and again, she'd noticed. Always would, she supposed as she was taken to another dark room and deposited inside it: onto the cold, stone floor.

'Ow... Watch what you're... No, wait! Don't leave me in here, I—' It was no use, the door was slammed shut behind her and those guards were gone.

There were more windows like those in the upstairs bedroom, but again they didn't let in any light... because there *was* no light. Instead, candles stood on stands and fought bravely against the darkness to allow her some vision. The room was in just as much of a state, more spiders' webs competing with rot and ruin. Curtains and tapestries were ragged and torn, more chairs that looked like they hadn't been used in decades and if they were to be now would simply collapse under the weight of a person.

But that wasn't all. She crawled forward. There, right there in the centre of the room, was a pit of some kind. An open space that people could be thrown into, that would deposit them into the dungeons of this place? Black, so black...

Marion scrambled back as the blackness shifted. As it moved, rippled. And it was only now, and as her eyes adjusted better to the light in this room, that she realised it wasn't an empty space at all. It had been filled with liquid of some kind. It looked like tar, thick and shiny, and as it bubbled she wondered for a moment if it might be hot. But no, as it *parted* she realised the mistake she'd made.

Because this liquid wasn't black at all. It was red. A deep, deep shade of red. The deepest actually, those ripples spreading out like the surface of a pond after a stone has been cast into it.

Then she saw the stone, though it was more like a boulder. And it hadn't been cast into this particular body of... not water, just what in the name of Herne was it? Hadn't been thrown in, so much as risen from its depths.

Not a boulder either, but a head. Pushing up and breaking the surface, causing more bubbles to appear and pop. The head was smooth, at the front at least, but the more of it that was revealed, the more Marion could see there was hair as well. Blacker than the liquid, beginning at the very top-point of the skull and flowing down; long, falling past the ears to shoulders that were also emerging.

The head, which was tilted slightly downwards, lifted – revealing a set of eyes first. Eyes Marion had to look away from, but then felt compelled to gaze into again seconds later. So intense were those eyes, she wanted to wrench her sight away a second time, but simply couldn't.

They were sheltered by a heavy, furrowed brow – beads of that liquid dripping from it to land on cheeks that were also slick with the stuff, which flanked an arched nose. Then a full mouth, a strong jaw-line. Next, a well-muscled body, rising as if being boosted from below. Broad-chested, arms like tree-trunks, legs looking like they were made from iron. The figure was totally naked, but covered in that dark-red substance – and now Marion could smell the coppery aroma of it, knew exactly what it was.

Blood.

He'd been bathing in blood – probably the blood of his enemies – was covered in it! Looked like he was walking across the surface of that pool towards her. And suddenly he was on the stone floor, still walking. The heat was rising to Marion's cheeks, and she was grateful when he covered himself with a loin-cloth. Then the man, who seemed even bigger than when they'd encountered him back in Sherwood – if that were possible – smiled, revealing brilliantly white teeth.

Marion had clambered to her feet, turned and started towards the door when a voice stopped her. 'No, stay!' it commanded. Then added: '*Please*, Marion. It is Marion, isn't it? There is nothing to be frightened of.'

It was such a strange thing to say, given what she'd just witnessed. But Marion turned around and faced him, jaw set firm.

'I'm not scared of you!' she said, though she couldn't hide the quiver in her voice.

'Then you will be the first. And yes, I could tell you were different when I first saw you. You have strength...' He walked a little further from the pool and Marion couldn't help backing away again. 'I apologise for neglecting you these past few days, but there was work to be done before the pleasure.' He held up his hand and she pulled a face at the way the liquid dripped slowly from his fingers.

'What? This? You disapprove?' He glanced back at the pool. 'Then you obviously do not know of the healing properties it boasts. That in some cases it can even... prolong life. Perhaps indefinitely. You will understand, eventually.' Dragos shook his head. 'I have been alone for such a long time. So long, you would not even believe...'

'I don't care!' said Marion, folding her arms over her chest.

There was a sudden rush of wind, something moving so fast it almost blew out the candles in that room. Then he'd covered the remaining distance between them, was staring down into her eyes. 'You will,' he promised her.

Marion felt woozy again, but this time it had nothing to do with the wound on her head, which was almost healed anyway. She twisted, looking first to the left, then the right. 'No,' she replied, but there wasn't much confidence in it.

'Do not fight it. *Look at me!*' Dragos held the sides of her head so she could not move it. 'I am... lonely. I need a bride, someone to share my new kingdom with.' Now he stroked her hair.

'A bride... a Red Bride?' she managed. 'For a Red Lord.' Marion took no small comfort in the way his face contorted when she said that name. She spat at him, and he sucked in a breath, surprised by her level of resistance. But it just made him redouble his efforts.

'Do. Not. Fight. Me!' With each word, she felt her energy being sapped. Until, finally, Marion slumped into Dragos' arms. '*Say it!*' he demanded. 'Let me hear you say it, my bride.'

Still she resisted, but in the end it was no use, she couldn't fight it anymore. Found, strangely, that she didn't want to. And so, very quietly, she whispered back: 'I belong to you now, my lord.'

He laughed, satisfied, and apparently genuinely happy – even though she'd had no say in the matter, wasn't choosing him of her own, free will. 'Good, good. Then tomorrow, Marion, we shall be wed!' he informed her and a part of her shivered. 'My blood to yours, my love…

'My blood, to yours.'

CHAPTER 14

Well, here they were, the attack scheduled for first thing that day – but they were waiting again.

And they weren't the only ones. Little John, on horseback, looked around him, at Robin and Tuck, Scarlet and Nasir all doing the same. And Much… Though John had been the first one to argue against the lad coming along – not least because none of them were sure he was really free of the Red Lord's control, regardless of what Herne said – Much had begged them to bring him. Needed to make up for what he'd done, he said. 'I didn't mean to. I want to help,' he'd said, eyes wet with tears.

Little John knew the boy better than anyone, had lived with him day-in, day-out in Hathersage, so in the end Robin had turned to him for the final say. 'Up to you, John. What do you think?'

Much had looked at him with those puppy-dog eyes, and he hadn't been able to refuse the young man. 'All right, all right. But we're keeping an eye on you!' Much had hugged him then, thanking him over and over. Besides, he told himself, even after everything that had happened, he trusted Much a lot more than the Sheriff, Guy or his any of his men.

The army Robin had 'found', or part of it anyway. John took that in now as well, more soldiers – some on horses, some on foot – as well as people from some of those villages that had been attacked, whoever was left… And Wickham. They'd sent as many bodies as they could spare as well, led by Edward, having come very close to tragedy themselves. 'If we don't fight,' he'd said, 'this will all find its way to us eventually.'

'Are you sure about this?' asked John then for what seemed like the thousandth time.

'What choice did I have?' replied Robin yet again.

John sighed, because their leader was right. He recalled what Robin had told them of the meeting with the Sheriff and Gisburne. A simple pact, though when was anything ever really simple where those two were concerned? An alliance, because they both wanted the Red Lord dead. Because *they* wanted Marion back safe and sound. They also needed men, so the Sheriff would lend them as many of his finest as possible. 'I'll even throw in Gisburne for free,' he'd apparently said and chuckled. It didn't exactly inspire confidence, but they needed the numbers. And they needed the location of Dragos' castle.

'We can't trust 'em!' Scarlet said now, and again not for the first time.

'I had no choice!' Robin repeated.

However, the closer to their destination they drew, slowly, creeping forwards, the more John began to think perhaps even with this army it wouldn't be enough.

'The Red Lord's definitely been busy.' Tuck gestured to the men both lined up outside the castle walls and on its walls. None of them were moving, though; nobody racing off to raise the alarm even though they could see what was approaching. The army that was slowly approaching, moving nearer to the castle with every moment. Holding steady, waiting for them to make a move.

A full frontal assault was really the only option they'd had with a structure such as this one, and with no cover for miles around it. But just because it was their only option, that didn't necessarily mean it was a good one.

'What are *they* waiting for?' asked Little John, when they were close enough to see the whites of their enemy's eyes – the majority of men there those in chainmail they'd seen back at Wickham.

'The puppet master to give the order,' answered Robin.

Then, when they were almost at the gate, the men immediately became animated, raising their weapons.

'All right, this is it!' Robin shouted. 'Remember the plan.'

'You play your part, wolfshead,' Gisburne called back. 'We'll play ours.'

Scarlet grunted. 'That's what I'm worried about.'

And then suddenly they were charging the castle.

***

Lord Dragos knew what was happening outside, but it was a mere inconvenience.

He had other matters to attend to, like his upcoming nuptials. It was a strange coincidence that the attack had come today, almost as if it was designed; the plan of some higher force. Naturally, he assumed it was the darker force that he served – which would enable him to wipe out what remained of the resistance in this area, at the same time he took his new spouse, thus allowing him to enjoy the hours, the days, months and years that would come after they were bonded to each other. Truly bonded, together always.

He'd craved her ever since the forest, had never seen such a magnificent creature as her. How she'd fought, the strength not only physical but in her will, her eyes! Dragos would have preferred for her to come to him of her own accord, to want this. But by the time the ancient ceremony was over, she would anyway. Marion would want, would desire no other...

The noise out there, the shouting, the clash of metal on metal – it broke into his thoughts, but he was content in the knowledge that it wouldn't last forever. The Sheriff's men, that little man in green who'd refused his offer... They were hopelessly outnumbered. Even if they managed to get through the wall of beguiled humans he'd put up to strengthen the castle's own, there were his personal guard waiting to face them, his chosen. Those people hadn't stood a chance in the forest against them. They wouldn't now.

All he had to do was wait again, Dragos had all the time there ever was.

And soon he would have someone to share it with.

Forever.

CHAPTER 15

Some of the men on the walls had bows and arrows, but they weren't the best shots with them – the projectiles hitting the ground in front of the horses.

The Sheriff's men, for their part, took aim with crossbows. A couple hit their marks and the men fell from the walls.

'No!' called out Robin. 'No killing, remember? They don't know what they're doing!'

He and his men were dropping down from their horses and engaging Dragos' forces outside the gate. One man swung at Robin and he arched, pulling in his stomach so the blow missed him and he wasn't sliced across the midriff. In retaliation, Robin punched him on the chin and the fellow went down. They might not feel pain in their current state, but that didn't mean it had no effect on their bodies.

'The torches!' Robin shouted back to the soldiers. 'Light your torches!'

A group of men carrying these came forward, thrusting them towards Dragos' troops – but the dark chainmail was simply protecting them too well.

Little John was doing the same and getting nowhere. 'It's no use, we can't get to the skin!'

'The necks!' Robin told them, their only vulnerable spot. 'Aim for the necks.'

But the rest were too busy defending themselves against the soldiers, against men who barely felt the wounds that were being inflicted on them. Scarlet had engaged in a swordfight with not one, not two, but three of the men, blocking blows to the left, then the middle and finally the right. When he fought back with his own thrusts, he tried to injure rather than kill – but they weren't repaying the favour.

'I... I think we're managing to hold them, though,' said Tuck, shouldering into one and sending him flying.

'Ya think?' cried out Scarlet, hardly convinced.

Nasir and Much meanwhile had made it to the wall, and were tossing up grappling hooks so they could climb the sides – the aim being to get beyond and open the gates from the inside.

But it didn't matter anyway, because moments later the gates opened on their own… releasing more troops, including those in black armour like the ones they'd encountered from the forest. Nasir's Al-ghul, the black knights. Their orders with regard to those poor unfortunates were to put them out of their misery if they could; that they were already beyond saving, so it would simply end their curse.

Out they spilled, the damned and the enchanted – like ants pouring from a hill. Now they really were outnumbered, the Red Lord having kept back even greater numbers to defend the castle.

Robin watched as one of the knights in black armour came at Little John, who kicked him back. The knight barely felt it, instead coming again at the larger man. John stepped to one side and grabbed him, swinging him around, at the same time pulling his helmet off. The knight growled with rage and charged again, only this time John brought up the end of his staff and whacked the side of his head with a crunching sound. Instantly, the knight stopped moving, then John grabbed him again and - heaving with all his might - he threw the knight into a couple more that were heading his way, knocking them over, pinning them to the ground.

Scarlet, meanwhile, was wrapping a length of silver chain around his closed fist. When one of the black knights came close enough, he roared and ran at the figure – ripping off the helmet himself and delivering a punch of his own. Scarlet struck again and again, until the figure was on its knees, then he unfurled the chain and wrapped it around the knight's neck, pulling back with all his strength, foot against the knight's back. Seconds later, the figure, clutching up at its throat, keeled over sideways and was still.

Nasir, who'd abandoned the rope he was going to use to climb, had found himself up against two of the black knights himself. They swung their swords, almost crossing them, and Nasir ducked to avoid these, sliding on the ground between the pair. When he rose, he crossed his own swords at the first knight's neck and pulled in opposite directions. While the knight's head was still flying into the air, he'd pivoted and swung with both his swords sandwiched together, decapitating the other as well. He saluted Robin with two fingers at the temple, grateful for the tip he had passed on from Herne about decapitation.

They were trying to buy him time, Robin knew. Hold off the fighters so that he could get inside the castle grounds. This needed to end, the most important link needed to be severed, and more than anything Robin wanted to get to Marion before anything happened to her. Herne might well have predicted that he'd lose her, but he didn't say anything about not getting her back again.

Some of the Sheriff's men were having a little luck with the flaming torches, jabbing them at the necks of the chainmail soldiers, although a few didn't seem to realise the difference between the ones just under the Red Lord's influence and those in the darker armour. Ones who could be saved and ones who couldn't. In the heat of battle, and fighting for their lives – wave after wave bearing down on them – Robin could understand the confusion, so the sooner he put a stop to this the better.

It was time…

Robin borrowed a torch briefly from one of the Sheriff's men and knelt, drawing a special arrow from his quiver and lighting the end. A flaming arrow, like the one he'd fired into the water to mark the passing of the previous Hood. Now, nocking that, his bow primed, he waved it left and right to keep any resistance at bay.

Light was the only thing the darkness understood, Herne had proved that if nothing else.

Using this, he created a path to the open gateway. Once or twice he heard attackers at his back, but by the time he'd turned, his own men had already taken them out. They were making sure all he had to worry about was what was ahead of him,

But that was enough, thought Robin.

More than enough.

CHAPTER 16

Robin had absolutely no idea where he was going, no idea how to find the Red Lord, or find Marion.

The castle ahead of him, just beyond the grounds, was big enough that it would take some time to search and by then it might be too late. He would just have to follow his instincts, he decided. That had always worked for him in the past, always brought him to Marion and she to him.

The fact that as he was making his way down a particular corridor, two more black knights – perhaps the biggest he'd seen yet – were waiting for him, blocking his path, told him he was probably on the right track this time as well. As they tended to do, they waited, silent and brooding, until he got closer to them. Robin still had his flaming arrow out ahead of him, but this didn't seem to deter them in the slightest.

He knew if he fired it, he wouldn't be able to light another quick enough, but did he even have time to do that before they sprung into action? One stepped forward, then *rushed* forward. It forced his hand and Robin had no option but to fire.

The knight braced himself, but the arrow simply glanced off the armour he was wearing. Robin dropped his bow, drew Albion, and he only just had time to meet the attack, metal clanging against metal. The knight pushed him backwards, strength almost matching the Red Lord's himself, but then Robin knew this particular pawn was just drawing on that same energy, evil empowering every move.

Now the other one joined his companion – a bearded man Robin saw, under the helmet – and brought his own sword down. It caught Robin on the top of his arm and immediately opened it up. Both of his opponents paused, seemingly mesmerised by the wound. It was just the distraction, the opportunity Robin needed, and he gripped Albion with both hands, swinging it round and catching the first knight at the neck. The sword bit deep, and then Robin had separated the head from the body; his blade sharper than any ordinary sword, moving like a hot knife through butter.

There was still one opponent left to contend with, though. And even as Robin looked around, he saw that knight's steel ready to cut him again. Ready to slice him apart in fact, and he couldn't do a thing about it.

'Look out!' came the cry. Then suddenly there was heat and fire in front of Robin's face, as a flaming torch was rammed up and under the remaining dark knight's helmet. His beard caught light, going up like fresh kindling, smoke billowing from under that helmet. The knight dropped, and lay still on the ground.

Robin couldn't believe it.

Then he saw the face of Much beside him, still holding the torch that had done so much damage. He was looking down with concern at Robin's arm, close to the shoulder, where he was bleeding.

'Are you all right?' he asked.

Robin nodded. 'It's not too deep.' Then he pulled the lad in close and thanked him. He asked to borrow the torch, which he ran along his wound, another use for it other than countering spells: this time to cauterise the cut and stem the blood-flow. Robin gritted his teeth, the pain incredible, but it needed to be done. 'Thank you,' he said again to Much when he was finished and his friend smiled at him.

'Now we can go and save Marion, can't we,' he said.

Robin nodded again. 'Now we can go and save Marion.'

Much helped him up and Robin retrieved his bow, which he slipped over his head to sit across his back. Then they left the two bodies behind, making their way up the corridor that had been blocked before.

'Where to now?' asked Much, and Robin pointed. Following his nose again, the sense that he was heading in the right direction. That if he just opened this door…

Darkness. That's what they saw when he pulled on the handle. But a living darkness, flowing out to meet them. He thought he heard Much yell out in terror, staggering backwards.

Robin brought up his free arm to shield his eyes, batting Albion back and forth. It was only when he heard the screeching that he understood what was happening. Winged creatures, black as the night, flying out through the doorway, hitting them, scratching and biting them.

'No… no, not *them!*' Much cried out, as if he'd seen these bird-like things before somewhere. He half-backed up, terrified, but was also being *pushed* back. Suddenly, he stumbled on a loose piece of masonry and fell.

'What are they?' Robin asked Much, but couldn't get any sense out of him. Robin didn't have a clue himself, he'd never seen their likes before – but he was willing to bet they had something to do with Dragos. That, like the damned and the lost out there on the battlefield, they were somehow under his control.

It was then that he found himself being pushed back by them as well., overwhelmed and consumed.

CHAPTER 17

In the throne room of the castle, Dragos cocked an ear and smiled.

'Can you hear that, my love? Our great day will be marked by bloodshed.'

'Bloodshed,' came Marion's slurred reply.

He'd dressed in crimson robes for the occasion and was holding Marion close to him. This room, like the one with the blood pool in it, was illuminated by a handful of candles and had yet more faded tapestries on the walls, long curtains framing barred windows that were not letting in any light, simply because there *was* no light to let in. Instead of the chairs, there was a carpeted area which led to a pair of thrones at the far end, larger and grander by far than the Sheriff's single one, but in more of a state of decay. Thrones for a king and for his queen.

'That's right. Our forces will soon be done with the intruders outside and later we will bathe in their blood to celebrate our first real victory. The start of everything, a new kingdom we will rule together! And to think that tiny Sheriff thought I was just interested in his money! In his petty squabbles... As for the intruders within, my pets will deal with them.' He let out a chuckle. 'But let us turn our attention to more important matters. You and I.' Dragos' fingernail trailed down Marion's cheek. 'When this is over, we will be as one.' He brought his mouth closer to hers, preparing for a kiss, only to find her pushing him away with her hands, then clenching her fists and beating his chest. 'No... no, my sweet. You have to let go. Forget your past, your old life. This must be done. Then you'll see. Let go of what you're holding on to. Let—'

'Why don't you do the same,' came a voice from the far side of the room.

Dragos looked up and over, seeing Robin standing there with his bow raised, an arrow trained on him. He was covered in scratches and bites, but otherwise unharmed. 'You! But...'

'Yes, *me*. Now let her go!'

Dragos reluctantly did as he was instructed, letting go of Marion so he could focus on this new threat. 'It matters not. She belongs to me. Tell him, my bride!'

'I... I belong to... to my Lord Drago,' Marion told Robin through gritted teeth.

'You belong to *no* man!' Robin said. Then he pulled back the arrow and fired at Dragos.

With incredible speed, the giant sidestepped the missile. Then he grabbed his sword which was propped up nearby, and swatted away the next several arrows fired, working his way towards Robin with each one.

The Hooded Man cast aside his bow and drew Albion instead, rushing to meet his opponent's attack. Their swords crashed together with an almighty clang, and this time Dragos felt more resistance than he had on that dirt track. Because this time, Robin was fighting *for* something – to get Marion back – and those feelings were giving him enormous strength.

Robin heaved him off and dodged a swipe, avoiding Dragos' sword, then managed to slip his blade through and nick the larger man's side. Dragos grunted and carried on swinging.

'You cannot win,' the huge man roared. 'In the end you'll be mine as well. You *all* will, one way or another!'

Robin met each one of the next blows delivered, until he was suddenly forced sideways and back, into one of the candle holders, which fell over onto the floor.

The light... Only light can defeat the darkness. Only the light can save us!

Struggling with the giant, Robin tilted Albion and caught the reflection of another candle, just in the right spot. The light seemed to magnify, intensify, and when it caught Dragos in the eyes – those wide, hypnotic eyes of his – he howled in pain before stepping backwards. Robin took the opportunity to slash him across the stomach as the man whipped his heavy sword left and right, hitting nothing, aiming blindly.

Then Dragos stopped still, pausing and waiting like one of those puppets he was in control of outside. He opened his mouth, dropping his weapon on the floor with another clang that echoed throughout the room.

Robin frowned, but seconds later saw why the man had halted. As the arrow that had been pushed into his back made its way through, out of his chest with a spray of red, as if the colour of his robes was suddenly running. He looked up at Robin, though it was unclear whether he could see him or not, then fell over sideways, clutching at the wound. Revealing Marion behind him, hands still up where she'd heaved the wood into Dragos.

Yet somehow the man was still alive, writhing around on the ground there. Robin drew closer, sword raised.

'Cut the head off the serpent,' he said under his breath. 'That would finish this…'

But before he could do so, a brightness filled the room. The clouds covering the sky outside seemed to vanish, letting in light: shafts of it through the barred windows. It was hard to tell whether it was the light that did it, or the fire leaping from the toppled candle which had ignited a carpet… but suddenly Dragos was on fire, the flames covering him like the ocean washing up on a beach.

That fire hopped from the floor to a set of curtains, and not long afterwards the whole room was ablaze.

'Come on!' Robin said to Marion, holding out his hand. 'Time to leave.'

They ran as Dragos' burning form reached a clawed hand out after them.

CHAPTER 18

Outside, Gisburne had already instructed his troops to pull back.

There was no point fighting men who apparently couldn't feel it when you struck them, or didn't seem to care – and though touching some of them with the torches did seem to do something, it really wasn't enough to stem the tide coming from that castle.

Then he saw it: the smoke, the fire coming from inside the walls, even as the sky up above continued to brighten. He'd spotted the wolfshead Hood venturing into the castle itself, followed by the simpleton and from what he was witnessing now, Gisburne had to assume that they'd been successful. That they'd somehow brought an end to the Red Lord's reign before it had even truly begun. And, yes, there was the wolfshead again, emerging with the 'lady' Marion, half-carrying the limping miller's son. His face soured at seeing them still alive, but then he remembered what he had to do. He had his orders: the part of the plan that Hood didn't know about.

Now, it was their turn to put an end to the outlaws' reign: Robin of Sherwood and his followers were about to be betrayed.

'Men!' shouted Gisburne. 'Now, while they're still distracted. Target the outlaws!'

***

Edward had been fighting one of the men in chainmail when he realised Gisburne and the Sheriff's men had turned on them.

They were firing crossbow bolts at him and the rest of Robin's band, racing towards them with swords drawn. Not only did they have to contend with the black knights, with the men in chainmail, now their original enemies had turned on them as well.

Nasir, Scarlet, Little John and Tuck were already taking them on as best they could, dividing their focus.

But something else was happening, Edward realised. The knights in black who looked like insects and those wearing the Red Lord's emblem had all stopped what they were doing. They'd frozen and were waiting again... but waiting for what exactly?

The man Edward had been fighting was now shaking his head, pulling off his helmet. 'What's goin' on?' he asked. Edward might have asked him the same thing.

'Is... isn't that Robin Hood and his men?' said another man wearing the red wings on his chest. 'And they need help. Look! The Sheriff's soldiers are attacking them!'

Now Edward understood, and especially when he saw Robin with Marion and Much. When he saw the flames coming from the castle. The Red Lord's hold on these men had been broken. The ones wearing the heavy black armour were all toppling over now, released, free of whatever black magic had been inside them, but the ones who'd simply been possessed... Why, they were joining forces now with their side *against* the Sheriff's troops.

Suddenly they had another army, a bigger army. And Edward couldn't help grinning at that, at the dawning realisation on Gisburne's face, waving and shouting for his men to retreat. 'Fall back! Fall back!' the coward was ordering, helpless against the sheer numbers of men who'd once been under Dragos' control.

On horseback and on foot, they fled. Turned around and ran off with their tails between their legs. Edward began cheering and soon Robin's forces joined in, as well as the others – some of whom didn't even really know what they were cheering for. It would be explained to them soon enough, that the battle against the Red Lord was over.

What Edward wasn't quite so sure about was how Gisburne would explain all this to the Sheriff. But he decided that, as fun as it would be to watch, he really didn't want to be around when that happened.

CHAPTER 19

They all watched from a distance as the castle went up in flames.

'Good riddance,' Much had said from his perch atop a horse, his ankle still too tender to walk on. Robin thought back now to when he and Marion had caught up with the lad, who was sitting on the ground behind the door - where Robin had dragged him out of the way of those winged things, slamming it closed again to keep them out. The young man had been so happy to see Marion. 'You're... You're all right!'

She'd smiled warmly. 'Yes, Much. I'm all right.'

'None of us will be if we stay here any longer,' Robin had told them and helped Much to his feet. They'd been reluctant to open the door again because of those flying beasts, but when they peered through a crack Robin saw they were just scattered about on the ground, as lifeless as those black knights now the Red Lord wasn't there to direct them.

The rest was history, getting to the gate and seeing the Sheriff's men had turned on them, only for the villagers Dragos had mesmerised to wake up and turn on *them*.

It was only now, as they waited there, watching, that Robin overheard some of the conversations. 'I'm... I'm not sure what happened,' said one boy, finally getting out of the chainmail he'd been wearing as one of the Red Lord's foot soldiers. 'I don't remember much at all... *Thomas*! I remember Thomas screaming, falling, but he... he...'

'What's your name, lad?' asked Little John.

'Jason,' he replied. 'I'm from just outside Lincoln.'

'Wait, I remember you! Didn't we help your village last winter?'

The boy nodded.

'Thought you looked familiar. You have family back there? Someone special?'

'I do… Sal, her name is. I-I think she's sweet on me.' He paused for a moment, then seemed like he wanted to admit something. 'I thought for a while that I wanted to join you, come on adventures. But now…' Jason shook his head.

'I don't blame ya,' Scarlet had said clapping him on the shoulder. 'Adventures are overrated. You're free now so you should get off to yer girl!'

'But *what* happened?' Jason asked again.

'The Red Lord,' Tuck told him. 'That's what happened.' The young man looked even more confused.

'It doesn't matter,' John added. 'You can go back now. *All* of you can.'

Not all, Robin thought. Some of them, the ones who'd been damned, cursed – like Jason's friend Thomas – were never coming back to the villages they'd been taken from, would leave loved ones to mourn them. Consumed by the flames back there, at least they were at peace now.

Spotting Marion, Robin waved and joined her. 'You weren't really going to become his bride, were you?' he asked.

She shook her head. 'I'm not sure I'm ready to be *anyone's* bride.'

Robin frowned. 'What, nobody's?'

'You said it yourself back there,' Marion replied with a playful smile on her face. 'I belong to no man.'

Robin rubbed the back of his neck. 'Well, that wasn't quite what… That's to say, what I meant was—'

Marion turned and kissed him on the cheek. Then she began to walk away.

The rest of his friends were there then, John ruffling his blond hair, and Scarlet jostling him, all of them laughing.

'Who's the puppet now?' joked John.

'All right, all right. I reckon it's about time we were heading off home too,' Tuck said then. 'Don't you? We might make it in time for dinner.'

John shook his head and chuckled again.

Robin nodded. 'Yes, home,' he said, looking up at the sky – at the bright sunlight above them. 'Back to Sherwood.'

And they all followed Marion off into the distance.

EPILOGUE

All was still in the castle.

The remains of the castle, that was – now the burnt out husk of a building. Nothing was moving, not even small animals or insects. It had been days since the battle, since the fire consumed everything. There was no wind rushing through the stonework, what was left of the corridors.

And yet something was answering the call. The same pull that had drawn a man to a forest so long ago and empowered him. The call of darkness, of evil. A bargain, and exchange.

In the throne room, the ash on the floor moved. Embers shifting. Only slightly, imperceptible to the naked eye. But they moved. No draughts were responsible, nothing natural at all. Nothing other than sheer will.

And a voice calling out, promising its servant they would have their revenge one day. That what was lost would be replaced, that they'd get it back. That time brings all things around again, situations repeating themselves – perhaps not even in this lifetime, whatever that meant for something which strived to be forever.

Saying the man of green *would* meet the man of red once more.

Whispering again and again: 'Nothing's forgotten... Nothing's *ever* forgotten.'

You may also enjoy...

Richard Carpenter's

ROBIN OF SHERWOOD

THE POWER OF THREE

Jennifer Ash

Richard Carpenter's

ROBIN OF SHERWOOD

THE MEETING PLACE

Jennifer Ash

www.ingramcontent.com/pod-product-compliance
Lightning Source LLC
Chambersburg PA
CBHW022045170626
46808CB00003B/1376